THE POWELL'S KITCHEN DOOR SQUEAKED OPEN.

Katie peeked from behind the line of towels as a tall man stepped onto the landing.

Scanning about as if finding his bearings, he walked slowly down the stairs. He had short, dark brown hair and sharp brows over a strong, straight nose. Broad shoulders filled the red polo shirt he wore untucked over loose khaki shorts, and he had long, muscular legs. At the bottom, he turned sharply, as if he knew she lurked behind the laundry. The strangest expression of longing filled his lean, intelligent face, and —

Complete déjà vu clobbered Katie as she raised her hand to give a neighborly wave. Pain warred with joy, strangling her greeting in her throat.

Matt? How could he be? Impossible, but this man had to be Matt. Katie pressed a hand over her wildly beating heart. Twenty years had passed, but the man was the spitting image of Edward Powell, Matt's dad.

Why on earth hadn't he come right over to say hello?

The delighted little girl in her burst through her shock and drove her bolting next door. She threw her arms around him. "Matt! Oh, it's so good to see you!"

Several impressions struck Katie simultaneously through her dizzy joy. Matt felt astonishingly different in her hug. Of course he did, he'd grown taller and filled out since their last summer together twenty years ago when she'd hugged a boy goodbye. This Matt was all man, and he fit her exactly how a man should, rocking her with a wild, weird surge of enthusiastic craving.

However, while the marvel of his presence and her abruptly resuscitated libido burst and bounced through her, realization dawned that he stood stock-still in her arms. He should be hugging her back. Why wasn't he hugging back?

Praise for Babette James

Summertime Dream

Summertime Dream is a perfect glass of Lemonade on a hot day. Simple, elegant and beautifully written. I enjoyed each scene. Loved the chemistry between the characters and the house. Great story! ~ Deborah Diez

Loved this sweet and sexy small town romance! Totally Recommend and Will Definitely look for more stories from Babette James! The scenes between Christopher and Margie range from sweet to steamy, and the secondary characters all add so much to the story. A little bit of house remodeling, a little bit of mystery and a whole lot of fun. I thoroughly enjoyed this story from start to finish. ~ Katie O'Sullivan

Family is of utmost importance in life for both characters in spite of their vastly different backgrounds. This makes their instant connection and love of solving a family mystery so enjoyable to follow. Their love of, and dedication to, fixing the house is a beautiful metaphor on the work relationships take, especially when broken, bloated, or forgotten. ~ InD'Tale Magazine (4½ Stars–Crowned Heart)

I loved this story! There were really 2 parts to it for me—the mystery of Christopher's great grandmother and the house she lived in, as well as the romance that developed between Christopher and Margie. The unveiling of the house in all its ancient glory was quite interesting to read, and equally as intriguing as the mystery of Christopher's family genealogy. I thought this plot line was quite unique and unfolded in a well written and engaging way. The romance between Christopher and Margie was sweet and tender and developed at just the right pace. The overall story was a fun, lighthearted read filled with tender moments and emotionally satisfying scenes. 5 delightful stars! ~ Maria Rose for RomCon Reader

Clear As Day

I truly loved how Ms. James expressed so well the emotional rollercoaster of their relationship. The fears, happiness, confusion and pain that Kay went through in coming to a decision of her next step to this relationship was expressed wonderfully. This book truly made me laugh, giggle and cry. If you want romance with all the emotions, whether good, bad or ugly, with some humor, this book is for you. ~ The Romance Reviews (5 Stars–Top Pick)

I loved not only the love story this book offered, but the dynamic of the side characters as well. I also fell in love with the emotional roller coaster this book took me on. ~ Insightful Minds Reviews

Though very sensual, this is still a sweet romance. ~ Romantic Times Book Reviews (4½ Stars)

My final thoughts are if you are looking for well written story that has just the right balance of sexy, love, and romance, this is a great story for you. ~ The Autumn Review

~*~

Books by Babette James

The River Series
Summertime Dream
Clear As Day

His Girl Next Door Series
Kissing Katie

I0530769

Kissing
Katie

His Girl Next Door - Book 1

by

Babette James

Chara Press

This is a work of fiction. Names, characters, places, and incidents are either the product of the author's imagination or are used fictitiously, and any resemblance to actual persons living or dead, business establishments, events, or locales, is entirely coincidental.

KISSING KATIE

COPYRIGHT © 2014 by Babette James

All rights reserved. No part of this book may be used or reproduced in any manner whatsoever without written permission of the author or Chara Press except in the case of brief quotations embodied in critical articles or reviews.

Cover Design and Interior Design by Jamie Banta
Images from Depositphotos.com

Chara Press
PO Box 281
Keasbey, NJ 08832

Visit Babette at www.BabetteJames.com

Publishing History
First Edition, 2014
Print ISBN-13: 978-0-9862513-0-6

Printed in the United States of America

Dedicated to

Grandma and Grandpa M
Love you and miss you both so much.
Thank you for all those lovely days at the shore.

~*~

The schooner near by sleepily dropping down the tide, the little boat slack-tow'd astern,
The hurrying tumbling waves, quick-broken crests, slapping,
The strata of color'd clouds, the long bar of maroon-tint away solitary by itself, the spread of purity it lies motionless in,
The horizon's edge, the flying sea-crow, the fragrance of salt marsh and shore mud,
These became part of that child who went forth every day, and who now goes, and will always go forth every day.

Walt Whitman, *There Was a Child Went Forth*

~*~

Chapter One

E'D COME HOME.

Matt Powell shook his head at that absurd thought and slowed the car as he took in his first sight of the old gray and white shore house standing unchanged on the corner.

He pulled into the wide driveway, the pale tan beach pebbles making the old familiar crunch under the tires. Still feeling tossed twenty years back in time, he glanced next door, past the low picket fence covered in clematis dividing the two driveways, slammed by the intense belief he'd see Katie out on the Vanburens' porch.

Pure wishful thinking, of course.

However, twenty-plus years ago, the boy he'd been would have, and he'd be unbuckling his seat belt and scrambling to escape his parents' car with a rushed, "Katie's there! Can I go? I'll be back in time for supper. I promise. Please?" With that, his summer vacation in Lavallette, New Jersey, and the best days of his life, would begin for real the moment his feet hit Katie's driveway.

Today, the big, shady screened-in porch wrapping the now-white house was empty, he and Katie had lost touch long ago, and the cheerfully painted mailbox read "MacBain." Katie was probably far away and married with a family these days. That's what she'd wanted back when they'd been best of friends forever.

A silver sedan stood in Katie's pebble driveway, and a rainbow of towels and clothing swayed on the clothesline. Besides the white siding, the new owners had renovated her old house with a tan shingled roof and summery blue trim, shutters, and lattice covering the porch crawlspace like a lacy skirt. Pink and white flowers overflowed the baskets hanging from the porch eaves and filled the garden beds.

He stepped from the car and filled his lungs with the hot, briny July air as he faced the shore house formerly owned by his grandparents. Nothing had changed. Still painted in faded battleship gray and white, the two-story home perched high on its concrete block foundation. Nana's favorite gaillardias splashed yellows and reds among the orange daylilies, and sun-bleached clamshells edged the flowerbeds and outdoor shower enclosure. The clotheslines gently sagged at the back end of the driveway over Nana's rosebushes.

Yes, he'd been looking forward to this vacation, but the upwelling sensation of coming home together with the rush of deep emotions and memories rocked him to the core. The feeling made sense. He'd been more at home here than anywhere else in his life.

Of course, the old house wasn't truly the same and never would be. Katie wasn't next door. Nana and Pop weren't waiting inside to ambush him with hugs, Dad wasn't ignoring Mom and sprawled out watching the Mets with Uncle Walt, Mom wasn't hiding on the porch with Aunt Dottie reading or working on her cross-stitch project, and Bruiser the cat wasn't lurking under the couch ready to attack passing feet.

Out of habit, Matt pulled out his phone. No voice mails. No e-mails. No messages. No appointments. Nothing.

Exactly what he wanted, exactly what he expected, yet still unsettling.

He'd just have to learn to relax again. He grabbed the house keys and two grocery bags and headed for the kitchen door. When this had been his family's house, no one used the front door except to fetch the mail.

Stepping into the stuffy, hot kitchen wrapped him further into the past. The same old pine cabinets lined the walls, and the same old table and chairs crowded the dining room. He inhaled, almost able to smell Nana's chicken casserole in the oven under the fresh wave of memories. A glossy new white stove and refrigerator replaced her old harvest gold appliances. Ordinary, sheer white curtains covered the lower window sashes. He dropped his load on the counter and headed outside to finish the rest.

With the car emptied, he opened a beer and took

a long sip.

Okay, he was officially on vacation. Retreat. Hiatus. Time out. Whatever. Calling these two weeks a vacation sounded better.

He set to unloading the cooler and the grocery bags, all healthy food—Except for the beer, of course. This was a vacation after all. He'd stuck to the eating healthier decision over the last few weeks, and he already felt better for the change. Major stress reduction had also helped.

Lizzie's ring tone warbled on his phone.

"Hey, sis."

"Are you there yet? I thought you would have called earlier."

"Traffic was heavy. I just arrived and unloaded the car. You wouldn't believe the place. It's like stepping back in time."

He opened cupboards and drawers. Old familiar dishes mixed in with new ones, and ordinary stainless flatware mingled with the timeworn silver-plate he'd used as a kid. He found two of the old cartoon-printed jelly glasses Lizzie and he had once used for their orange juice at breakfast. Nana's old electric percolator sat tucked on a shelf.

He laughed. "Even some of Nana and Pop's dishes and flatware are still here."

"That's so weird. I still can't believe you went back to Lavallette when you could have chosen Aruba or Hawaii, or some other fun place. Somewhere with air conditioning and room service?"

"I don't need fun. I just need to relax."

Her voice softened, and her concern warmed her words. "I know. I know. How's your stomach doing?"

"Much better. And that's not a get-my-big-sister-off-my-back deflection either. I haven't needed the pills for a week."

"That's great. I'm happy for you. So, give me a tour. What's new, what's old?"

"They left the pine beadboard walls unpainted. The living room furniture is new, except for the red bookcase and the corner side table. Pop would have liked this flat screen TV."

The place had cable now, so he could enjoy catching a baseball game or two. Still no AC in the house, which the rental agent had apologized for, but that lack was fine by Matt. If he'd wanted fancy amenities, he'd have gone to a resort. He was here for the rest and the memories.

"So, which bedroom will you stay in?"

A good question. Definitely not his old stuffy digs upstairs once shared with his older cousins, Dirk and Greg. Lizzie had been squeezed in with Tricia, Lana, and Briana, but at least the girls were all close in age and had gotten along. Dirk, Greg, and he still had nothing in common but an impersonal exchange of Christmas cards.

He peeked into his uncle and aunt's old room. Same old furniture, plump new mattress.

"Uncle Walt and Aunt Dottie's room in the back will be quieter."

True enough, but Nana and Pop's room in the front offered a view of the bay and caught the breezes best on a hot night.

"Whoa. Nana and Pop's old mahogany bed and dressers are here, too."

"Please tell me it's not the same mattress."

The smooth stretch of the summer-weight bedspread proved this bed also had a firm new mattress. Nana and Pop's mattress had always had two gently sagging hollows worn over the years and napping on their bed had been like sleeping in a hammock.

"Nice and new."

"Thank goodness for that."

"The bathroom was renovated."

The fixtures he'd known had been originals from 1934, so that update was a welcome change.

Upstairs, little had changed in the three bedrooms beyond new beds.

Most nights, rather than endure his unwelcoming cousins, the airless room, and the creaky fold-up bed with the weird spring, he'd slept curled on the porch chaise lounge until dawn woke him and Nana. She'd make him a milky, sugary cup of coffee, and they'd play solitaire together until Pop woke. Then she'd start breakfast, and he'd share the newspaper with Pop. The rest of the family always slept in late, so his mornings were sweet and peaceful, and he had Nana and Pop all to himself.

The boys' room held the attic hatch door, and he couldn't resist peeking in and pulling the chain for the light.

"The attic's full—the old towel trunk, beach chairs, crab cages, canoe paddles, fishing nets, a seine net, and a laundry basket full of beach toys. I wonder if the canoe is still under the house. Maybe I'll go crabbing while I'm here."

"Crabbing? You're kidding, right?" Her laughter pealed over the phone. "Oh! Are the Vanburens still next door?"

"No. There's a new name on the mailbox. MacBain. The place looks good though."

"Have you ever thought about trying to get in touch with Katie again?"

He shrugged, wincing at the sharp pinch of remorse and loss. Undeniably, he should have done so years ago—he should never have let life's troubles break them apart in the first place. Anyhow, he'd probably let things go too long to bother tracking her down now, like the failed connection with his cousins. "It's been twenty years. I'm sure she's forgotten all about me."

"You should consider it. What do you have to lose? Someone in the neighborhood might still be in touch with her family."

"True." He walked out to the porch and studied the thunderclouds churning their way up into billowing pillars beyond the sparkling bay. Another wave of sentimental happiness rose over his remorse, and he smiled. Katie and he'd always loved watching the summer storms roll across Barnegat Bay.

Seagulls wheeled over the blue water dotted with sails, and pairs of people scattered the docks, crabbing and fishing. Families with small children filled the little beach, enjoying the warm, kid-friendly shallows and the playground. A modern, bright red, yellow, and blue climbing contraption stood in place of the swings and old steel merry-go-round of his childhood.

"So, what are you going to do first?"

"Finish my beer and unpack my suitcase. Looks like we'll have a thunderstorm come through soon. Maybe I'll take a walk up to the boardwalk afterwards."

"You'll die of boredom in a day."

"I always found plenty to keep me busy when I was here."

"You were a kid then, doing kid stuff. I don't see you playing on a boogie board or building sandcastles for two weeks."

"Lizzie, I'm here to relax, do nothing, and enjoy a distraction-free space to make a decision on the offers."

Quitting without having accepted the next job was unsettling and weirdly freeing. He only regretted the impulsive decision on the occasional nights of insomnia. He had three equally excellent offers, and each firm wanted him strongly enough to wait patiently on his answer. Nice being a sought-after commodity.

"Well, at least you're close enough to New York and Atlantic City if you do get bored. I only wish you were moving closer, not further away. I understand they're all great offers, but . . ."

"That's what planes are for. I'll visit you and Julia just as often, maybe even more. I'll have more time—"

Lizzie's laughter cut him off. "Promises, promises."

"You could always pack up and move east with me. You'd make more money."

"I'm not uprooting Julia, and you wouldn't want that for her either."

"She's four and happy, so a move for her wouldn't be even remotely like what happened to us. Anyhow, we adapted."

Lizzie snorted. "N. O., brother dearest. Okay,

I've got to run. Lots to do. Julia has her swimming lesson, and I have a date tonight. Wish me luck, enjoy your quiet, and call occasionally."

"Good luck. I will. Hug Julia for me."

He finished his beer and pocketed his keys. He'd walk to the end of the docks, stretch his legs, and breathe some salty bay air to jumpstart him on clearing the crap out of his head.

~*~

Katie stepped outside, propping the laundry basket on her hip, and sighed happily at another lovely, hot summer Saturday at the Jersey shore. Hopefully the towels were dry and ready for folding since the usual afternoon thunderheads piling up on the horizon looked promising. She always enjoyed a good thunderstorm.

Next door, a snazzy luxury sports car gleamed in the Powell's driveway. She still thought of the old house as the Powell's although they'd sold the place ages ago.

Since the new renters had parked squarely in the driveway, rather than tucking neatly to the side to make room for other cars, perhaps they were just a couple, rather than a family or group. Katie crossed her fingers against music-blasting partiers. The rental agent was on top of screening, so most of the time she was happy with her temporary neighbors.

She plucked off the first clothespins, dropped them into the basket, and folded the towel.

Maybe after the storm passed, she'd walk up to the Seaward Inn and read a book over a nice dinner of crab cakes and glass of wine to celebrate, well, the beautiful day. She was all caught up on work and had her home to herself today. She loved family stopping by, adored the days when the house groaned at the seams with her parents and her brother's and sister's families, but she also liked her peaceful, private days.

The Powell's kitchen door squeaked open.

Katie peeked from behind the line of towels as a tall man stepped onto the landing.

Scanning about as if finding his bearings, he walked slowly down the stairs. He had short, dark brown hair and sharp brows over a strong, straight nose. Broad shoulders filled the red polo shirt he wore untucked over loose khaki shorts, and he had long, muscular legs. At the bottom, he turned sharply, as if he knew she lurked behind the laundry. The strangest expression of longing filled his lean, intelligent face, and —

Complete déjà vu clobbered Katie as she raised her hand to give a neighborly wave. Pain warred with joy, strangling her greeting in her throat.

Matt? How could he be? Impossible, but this man had to be Matt. Katie pressed a hand over her wildly beating heart. Twenty years had passed, but the man was the spitting image of Edward Powell, Matt's dad.

Why on earth hadn't he come right over to say hello?

The delighted little girl in her burst through her shock and drove her bolting next door. She threw her arms around him. "Matt! Oh, it's so good to see you!"

Several impressions struck Katie simultaneously through her dizzy joy. Matt felt astonishingly different in her hug. Of course he did, he'd grown taller and filled out since their last summer together twenty years ago when she'd hugged a boy goodbye. This Matt was all man, and he fit her exactly how a man should, rocking her with a wild, weird surge of enthusiastic craving.

However, while the marvel of his presence and her abruptly resuscitated libido burst and bounced through her, realization dawned that he stood stock-still in her arms. He should be hugging her back. Why wasn't he hugging back?

Because it's been twenty years, and he has a wife or girlfriend in the house watching you make a fool of yourself with her man.

Oh, no! She snatched her hands off him and leapt back a step, only to bump into his car. She glanced up to see if anyone was watching them from a window.

Matt's startled gaze swept over her, a shifting tangle of confusion and male appreciation. "Uh . . . You know me?"

That puzzlement broke her heart. How could the most important friend from her childhood have forgotten her? She'd never forgotten him, although she'd honestly never expected to see him again. Except now he was here, more handsome and wonderful than she could have ever imagined he'd become, even back in the blithe childhood days of make-believe when she was his mermaid princess, and he was her daring prince.

"Of course."

Then he blinked, and his brown eyes flew wide. "Katie?" He scanned her again, disbelief flaring to shock. "Holy shit! Katie, it's really you?"

A tidal surge of joy washed away the hurt. "It's

me, all grown up."

"Damn, it's great to see you again." He shook his head. "This is such an incredible surprise."

She laughed. "I know. You must have wondered who this crazy woman was running toward you."

"My mind was totally elsewhere until you called my name and tackled me. How have you been?"

Unable to restrain herself, she hugged him again, and this time he hugged her tight before letting go.

"Oh, I can't believe you're here. Oh, my gosh! This is awesome. I keep thinking I should pinch myself.

Matt was here! After his parents' divorce, Matt's mom had taken Matt and his sister to Colorado and never let him return to New Jersey. She'd never stopped missing Matt, even after he'd stopped writing, and she'd resigned herself to his only being a precious happy memory.

"You're staying here? But your grandparents sold it."

"I needed a vacation and on a whim decided to see if I could rent the place. I lucked out, and here I am."

"How long are you staying?" She glanced at the house. "Are you here with friends, wife, girlfriend?"

"Two weeks." He shrugged and shifted edgily, as if he were uncomfortable with small talk. "No wife. No girlfriend. Just here by myself for some long-needed rest and relaxation."

He cast a fleeting look at her bare left hand before he nodded his chin toward her house. "The house looks great."

"I've spiffed up the inside, as well. Making the

place mine has been great fun."

"Yours?"

"I bought the house from my parents three years ago, and I'm living here year round."

"That's great."

"I couldn't be happier. My family invades almost every weekend, but I love the company. In fact, my parents are coming down tomorrow. They'll be so happy to see you again. We all missed you so much."

"Be nice to see them again."

Katie puzzled over his flat politeness. That wasn't the Matt she knew. He seemed . . . subdued and on-edge. Maybe he was simply tired after a long trip from, well, from wherever he was from these days.

He eyed her mailbox, definitely puzzling over the name.

Her stomach twisted into an aching knot, and she braced for the inevitable questions. She should have replaced that mailbox years ago, but Marie had painted it and wouldn't understand.

~*~

Katie, all grown up. Still his Katie, but holy shit, had she grown up nice.

Still reeling from surprise, Matt kicked himself for not instantly knowing Katie by her happy run and shout of his name. He'd been lost in thoughts of the past, and before he could focus on the now, she'd plastered herself around him in that enthusiastic hug. Her soft curves had hit him in all the right places and intellect had been momentarily derailed by an out-of-the-blue punch of pure lust.

Lust. For Katie? For his once upon a time best

friend forever? He blinked.

Katie. Same sun-streaked toffee brown hair. Same pretty, bright blue eyes, but no longer hidden behind thick glasses. Same cheerful, dimpled smile, but she'd undergone the same torture of braces as he had. No longer a gawky, reed-slender slip of a girl, she'd filled out real nice—

Heated guilt rushed over him at how part of him was busily considering how nicely her breasts would fill his hands.

He shook his head. Katie, with *breasts*.

Katie had always just been Katie, his best friend. Now there was no ignoring she was all woman. Her sleeveless, summery dress hugged trim soft curves and long tan legs, and the deep V of the bodice discreetly emphasized her perfect breasts. Pink painted toenails peeped out from the silly bright flowers decorating her sandals.

Katie had breasts, and he was standing dumbstruck with a hard-on for his former best friend, praying she didn't notice.

And he was missing what Katie was saying.

"—Would you like to come over? If you don't have other plans, I'd love to catch up, find out what you've done with your life. Wow, I can't believe you're here."

This reunion had to qualify as the weirdest and most disconcerting moment in his life. He paused too long gathering his wits before answering, and the happiness in her face faded.

Tell her yes. Vacation, remember? No hurry. No worries. What better way to kick off a vacation at the shore than with Katie? Just like old times.

"Sure, yes, I'd like that. My only plans were to

walk out to the dock before the storm rolls in and to unpack."

The sparkle returned to her eyes, and a warm rush filled his chest.

"The rain might miss us. You never know, but I was taking in the laundry, just in case."

"Want me to give you a hand with the rest?"

Katie glanced over at the line, her cheeks coloring. Beside the towels and the swimsuits, a rainbow of lacy underwear waved in the breeze.

He grinned. "How about I'll get the towels and let you handle the rest."

"Ah, okay, thanks."

The MacBain name on the mailbox, but no ring on her hand bugged him. Might as well come straight out and clear up the issue right now.

"So, any significant other?"

As if jabbed by pain, Katie sucked in a deep breath and glanced away before she spoke. "No one now. I was married. That's why the mailbox says MacBain. Jeb passed away four years ago."

Oh, crap. A whole wave of sorrow and worry for her slammed him.

"I'm so sorry."

"Thanks." She smiled thinly, failing to veil her pain, and picked up the laundry basket.

As Matt tackled the towels, he struggled to process Katie's news. Katie. Here. Sexy. Beautiful. Married. *Widowed.*

Conflicting impulses yanked and wrestled within him. Hold her. Escape.

Worse, the news left him nonsensically imagining he'd let her down in some way even more than he had as a boy, that somehow he should have been there for her, should have fixed her pain.

His mind soared back twenty-five years to their first meeting. He'd been hanging at the playground fence, lonely and grumpy, ditched by his older cousins, who'd taken off for Seaside, and by Lizzie, who'd rather take knitting lessons from Nana.

Katie had been struggling to push the big steel disk of the merry-go-round by herself, skinny legs churning over the sand, and then jump on to ride the lackluster spin. She'd heave a sigh, jump off, and gamely restart the whole routine.

"You're not big enough." That sour thought shot from his mouth. "You'll never get it going fast by yourself."

She paused to eye him and pushed a finger at the bridge of her glasses. "I can try. I'm getting better at it."

With a toss of her sun-bleached hair, Katie clenched her jaw, tightened her grip on the handrail, and shoved, huffing and puffing as she jogged. The slippery, soft sand made digging in her feet and getting the leverage she needed difficult. Her green flip-flops weren't helping.

He sauntered over, as much as a scrawny eight-year-old could saunter on sand in stiff, new sneakers. The other kids playing around the beach and on the swings were even younger. She'd get no help from those babies.

Loping into a jog behind her, he caught a rail and heaved his own spindly weight into the job. Her laughter pealed as they sped along faster and faster.

"One, two, three. Jump!" Katie swung her legs up, losing one flip-flop.

After a hard last push, Matt jumped on, and

they hung on tight, laughing through the dizzy spin.

The merry-go-round slowed into lazy rotation, and she scooted around to face him and sit cross-legged.

"That was great! Hi, I'm Katie. You're one of the Powell's, right? I've seen you there. Except, you're new."

"I'm Matt. Yeah, we usually only visit Nana and Pop at Christmas, 'cause we live in California, and Dad's always too busy."

"My grandparents own the house next door. We're the Vanburens. How long are you visiting?"

"The whole entire summer," he said glumly. "Lizzie and I are supposed to get to know our cousins. Except they don't want 'the little runt' hanging around."

"Pretty much the same problem here, only we come here all the time, and I already know them." She rolled her eyes. "I get to be here all summer, too. I love staying with Grandma and Grandpa, but always being the littlest is a huge pain."

"Yep."

They'd both been weedy and stick-thin then, the runts of the litter in their respective families. Their older teen siblings and cousins—conveniently forgetting their own recent weedy stages of life—had made Katie's and his second-class station in life miserably clear.

She grinned and pushed up her glasses. "I'm eight. How about you?"

"I'm eight too."

"Perfect! Do you like crabbing?"

"Never done it." He hated admitting he didn't know how, but he'd seen the people on the dock, and he wanted to learn.

"I can show you. It's easy, if you're patient. Let's push this thing again and see if we can go even faster." She pinned him with her dimpled grin and jumped off.

From that moment, they'd stuck to each other like glue all summer and all the following years until his battling parents had broken his family. What had started out as the worst summer in the world became the five best years of his life.

Having a girl best friend didn't bother him one bit. They liked the same stuff: fishing, crabbing, boogie boards, snorkeling, riding bikes, and checking out piles of worn paperback books from the library where they discovered Jules Verne, Edgar Rice Burroughs, C.S. Lewis, and J.R.R. Tolkien, and telling each other long, fanciful stories that they jotted into flimsy notebooks. Katie and he had spent their allowance at the ice cream shop, the bait shop, and their favorite shop of all: the variety store crammed with every bit of summer vacation treasure, junk, and candy a kid could desire.

"So where are you living now?"

Katie's question dragged him into the present. "At the moment, Seattle, but I'll be moving soon."

"Wow, with all the gorgeous places to visit out west, you came all the way here just for a vacation at the shore?" She dropped the last folded top into the basket. "All set."

"Seemed like a good idea at the time. Lizzie thinks I'm crazy too." He grinned and lifted the laundry basket. "Where would you like this?"

"Follow me." She led him through the side porch door into the bright updated kitchen. "You can just leave the basket on the table there. I'll deal with it later. Let's sit on the porch. I want to know everything. Would you like something to drink? Water, soda, tea, wine?"

"Water's good, thanks."

Out on the front porch, sturdy wicker furniture with comfortable cushions replaced her grandparents' worn and haphazard collection of decades ago.

Katie curled up on the couch, and he took the chair opposite.

The sensual attraction to Katie remained baffling and captivating. She'd been a cute kid. Now she was a lovely woman, but they were no longer kids, and part of him was taking fascinated notice of that fact and her single status. Worse, notwithstanding the escalating potential for embarrassment, certain really imprudent parts of him had enthusiastically embraced the situation and had yet to take no for an answer.

He took a long swallow of the cold water. No doubt about it, this vacation was going to be very interesting.

Chapter Two

KATIE SIPPED AT HER GLASS OF WATER, STILL dizzy with the excitement of Matt's return and the lingering heat of need their hug had sparked off. "So, where are you moving?"

His brows rumpled into a troubled line, and his lips pressed thin. "Not sure yet. I'm considering three offers. Depending on the firm I choose, either D.C., Richmond, or Atlanta. I'll be making my decision by the end of my stay here."

"What kind of job are you considering?"

"I'm an attorney. I've been offered partnerships at three law firms."

"Wow. That's great. Do you know which one you want to accept?"

"They're all excellent, each with their own tempting pluses, as well as their own individual minuses. In all cases, the pluses far outweighed the minuses, making the decision difficult. I could accept any one and be very happy, but I decided not to rush into a decision. I'll give them my answer at the end of these two weeks. How about you? What career did you go into?

"Well, I have my own business. I create websites and offer a whole variety of graphics design and web services for my clients. I love it."

"Sounds like fun and a good challenge. I wish you the best."

"Thank you. Setting out on my own was definitely a scary challenge in the beginning, and those oh-my-what-on-earth-was-I-thinking days still occasionally hit, but I love working from home, and I'm very happy I took the leap. I'll show you my office and some of my work later, if you like."

"I'd like that." That familiar boyish grin lit his face. "I would have guessed you'd become a writer or a journalist. You were always dreaming up stories."

"Well, I loved my art too. When I hit computer art and design in high school, I fell completely in love with the possibilities, and I knew exactly what I wanted for a career. What about your own writing? Your stories were always better than mine, all mystery and exciting grand adventure."

Matt shrugged and took a long draw on his water. "Just one of those things left behind, I guess."

He'd said no wife or girlfriend here with him, but he could still have one lurking in Seattle. Time to clear that up.

She gathered a settling breath. "How about you? Any significant others past or present? Children?"

"No wife or even ex-wife. A few ex-girlfriends

here and there over the years. Just haven't met the right one for forever yet. Someday . . ." He shrugged. "No children either. I always thought I'd like a kid or two of my own down the road. I have a niece, Julia. She's four, cute as a button and smart. Do you want kids? I mean, I remember you did when we were kids talking about that someday-when-we're-grownup kind of stuff."

Katie rolled the glass between her hands and glanced at her bare ring finger. Being the only one at family gatherings without a spouse and a child hurt.

"I wanted kids, still do, but Jeb wanted to wait and enjoy a few more years of fun before we settled into parenthood. We were young. Fun seemed reasonable at the time."

If they'd only known . . .

She raised a smile for Matt. She refused to be a downer on this happy day.

"I've started dating again, on and off."

Well, more off than on, and no one seriously, but she'd begun moving on with her life, that was what was important.

"So there's still hope of a family someday."

"Again, I'm so sorry."

The sorrow for her in Matt's eyes and voice made her want to wrap her arms around him and promise him she was okay. "Thanks."

She was sorry, too. No matter her anger with Jeb, he'd been far too young to die. A terrible waste. He'd been fun and intense, thoroughly derailing her common sense when they'd met and all through and after their whirlwind courtship. He'd loved her truly, madly, deeply, and she'd loved him the same to the end.

Unfortunately, Jeb's death had also revealed that his life's motto was apparently 'Love the one you're with' and she hadn't been the only one he was loving.

Tears pricked.

Stop. No crying over spilt milk.

"Would you like some pretzels? I feel like having some pretzels."

"Thanks."

Out in the kitchen, she pulled herself together as she filled a bowl with a mix of pretzels and crackers and pulled out the new goat cheese dip.

She was fine now. Life was good.

Thunder grumbled in the west.

"Looks like we'll be getting that storm. I haven't tried this cheese dip yet. Let me know what you think."

She set the snacks between them on the wicker coffee table. Food and weather were safe topics to breach the quiet gaping between them, right?

Folks on the docks and on the little beach bustled to clear out as the sky darkened and lightning danced over the far shore.

The storm rolled swiftly across Barnegat Bay and the skies let loose. A pounding deluge beat on the roof and hissed over foliage and gravel. Bright lightning flashed and sharp retorts of thunder cracked.

"I won't need to water the garden tomorrow. This one will fill up the storm drains." She took a long sip from her glass as Matt took a taste of the dip.

Matt grinned. "Thumbs up on the dip. Remember us always being in a hurry to wade in those huge puddles, and how warm the water got from the street?"

A rush of happy memories filled her with laughter. "And remember how my mom always yelled at us to stay out of that dirty water?"

"Is she still as germ phobic?"

"Oh, yes. I don't know how she ever survived our childhood and teaching preschoolers."

"Is she still teaching?"

"Mostly retired. She subs for the private school near their home. Dad's still working. Mom says he can't retire or she'll have to go back to full-time, because he'll make her nuts being underfoot all day."

The drumming rain slackened into a gentle lingering shower.

Talking with Matt was so easy, just like old times. They slipped from topic to topic, sharing news of their families, accomplishments from their high school and college years, favorite vacations, both of them firmly sticking to fun, happy memories, and judiciously skirting around his parents' divorce and her marriage.

The storm passed, afternoon eased into evening, and Matt accepted her offer of supper and helped in the kitchen. Their conversations rambled on through roast chicken and a bottle of wine and a hot orange sunset, and then ice cream out on the porch, until the night was dark and late.

She hugged him tight with goodnight kiss to his cheek, and he wrapped her in a sturdy, heartfelt embrace, returning the brushing kiss. However, that small innocent contact added a new layer of confusion to the unsettling sensual attraction still simmering from their first hug.

"Goodnight."

"Sleep well. See you tomorrow."

As Matt walked next door, Katie sighed and made herself turn and go inside. Telling Matt about Jeb had churned up the conflicted feelings she still had for Jeb. She'd loved the sweet philandering idiot so intensely, and she honestly missed him and the good times they'd shared. How could she not?

Back when they'd met, she'd been working too hard and harried with college courses. Jeb had showered her with attention and affection and been the breath of fun and adventure she'd needed in her life. Jeb had been a dedicated firefighter and Little League coach, giving of his time and energy—a big, generous kid, really. The sole solidly responsible act Jeb had done for their short marriage was his life insurance policy. Thanks to his spontaneous husbandly moment, she now owned the house she loved.

However, the embarrassment and anger remained as strong as her sorrow. There were times after the funeral, after she'd learned about Jeb's cheating, when she'd wondered if he'd ever meant to keep his promise of a family. If only he'd been as scrupulous with his vows as he'd been with contraception.

She prayed Mom and Dad restrained any impulse to fill Matt in on the sorry side of her marriage. They'd been furious for her and were less than discreet in speaking their minds in the matter as she'd prefer.

As for telling Matt herself—well, at this point in their reunion, bringing up that humiliation was an item she'd like to avoid permanently. She squelched the silly urge to call and ask them to come another day.

Missing Jeb was okay, grieving the man she'd loved was okay, and hopefully, someday she'd find forgiveness for his faults, but she had regained her commonsense and learned her lesson.

She would absolutely, positively never let herself be blindly swept off her feet again by any man.

~*~

As Matt let himself into the dark, stuffy house, the warm light from Katie's house tempted him to escape the emptiness here and return to her company.

He paced around the house, opening windows to the warm night breeze.

After unpacking, he stripped and flopped into bed, but his mind was spinning too much to settle. He opened an e-reader app on his phone.

Today had been so unexpectedly great. He'd enjoyed hanging out with Katie and talking as if the long years separating them had been erased, and he'd appreciated the temporary diversion of some of the weight and stress on his mind.

Mostly. Sorrow for the grief she'd endured through losing her husband shadowed his pleasure. Definitely not an outcome they'd covered in their childish dreams. At least she'd begun to date again. Beautiful, smart, and fun, she'd find someone to love her again.

As for his disconcerting, intriguing, intense physical attraction to her as a woman . . .

He groaned. This was a problem. She was *Katie*.

A loud burst of birdsong jarred him upright from a fuzzy dream. He caught his phone before it tumbled off the bed. Rolling over, he took a deep breath of cool morning air and squinted at the clock.

Five after five. So much for sleeping in on his first morning of vacation. The early bird mockingbird in the maple outside his window warbled stridently as if to agree.

He chuckled and stretched, yawning. What to do first? Having nothing planned was an uncommon state of being in his life.

He shook his head and pushed out of bed. Today was Sunday, and he firmly intended to make following his whims the only item on his schedule.

Time for coffee. Then, since he was on a nostalgia trip, he'd walk up to Dorsey's Bakery for the Sunday paper and a couple crumb buns.

Donuts and crumb buns on Sunday mornings had been a breakfast tradition of his grandparents. He'd been so proud when Pop trusted him to make the errand, bills crinkling in his pocket on the walk there, change jingling on the trip back as he carefully balanced the heavy pastry box and thick Sunday paper.

Life was so simple then: be on time for lunch and supper, no whining, make your bed, don't track sand in the house, no going up to the ocean by yourself, rinse out your bathing suit and hang up your towel, help Pop weed the yard, and help Nana dry the dishes.

After filling the coffee carafe, he paused, flooded with childhood images of mornings with Nana. He set aside the carafe and pulled out the ancient percolator. A twist tie replaced the cord holder made by Lizzie out of a toilet paper roll, a paper lace doily, and construction paper hearts. Strange how he remembered the routine to setting up the old thing. Would the coffee taste as good as his memories promised? Nana had always loaded his mug with milk and sugar. He couldn't drink his morning brew that sweet and milky these days, but he'd always loved her percolated coffee.

He waited until the percolator's first whooshing burp confirmed the old pot still worked before heading into the bathroom to wash the sleep from his eyes and to shave. He reached for the razor, and then laughed at himself in the mirror. Vacation was in effect. He'd shave later today, or tomorrow, and add a small, progressive break from routine.

How else could he break from routine?

He glanced at the television. Okay, he could go no news. His laptop sat on the TV table. No e-mail or social media. A variety of paperbacks crammed the old red bookcase. No e-reader. He could handle unplugging from the world for a day.

Quiet from the kitchen signaled the coffee was ready. He fixed his coffee with milk and a small amount of sugar and took a first sip. Pretty damned perfect.

Sipping at his coffee, he perused the five shelves of paperbacks and found a new mystery to read out on the porch. The redwood chaise lounge that had once served as his bed for countless nights was gone, but the new porch sofa was comfortable, and he stretched out and propped his feet up on the creaky wicker coffee table.

His view west across the bay was picture-perfect and peaceful, the sky a cloudless pastel blue, the water of the bay flat and calm, and the cool air promising a beautiful day. A jogger ran past. A few minutes later, a dog walker strolled into view, patiently pausing every few yards as his energetic beagle examined each weed and tuft of grass along the median of Bay Boulevard.

Several chapters and two mugs of coffee later, his stomach growled. Time for crumb buns. Fixing a bowl of cereal would be faster, and healthier, but he could have cereal tomorrow morning.

When he stepped out the kitchen door, he spotted Katie curled on her porch sofa with a paperback in one hand and a coffee mug in the other.

He waved and walked around the fence.

She pushed at the wire-rimmed glasses slipping down her nose and waved back. "Good morning. You're up early. I guess you're still a morning person."

Chuckling, he nodded. "Still am. I'm heading up to Dorsey's to get the newspaper and some crumb buns."

She looked sweet and rumpled in her blue tank top and soft knit shorts, as if she'd just rolled out of bed. This was likely, considering it was barely six thirty in the morning.

Oh, hell, and she was braless under that thin top. An inviting image of her waking in his bed sucker-punched him, and his body tightened.

Scrambling for a change of thought, he jammed his hands into his pockets. "You wear glasses?"

Brilliant. What are you? Eight again?

Being eight would make life so much simpler.

Katie just smiled. "Sadly, yes, I still need them. I

was wearing my contacts yesterday."

"Ah, want to walk with me?"

Where had that blurt come from? Was he channeling his kid self again? She'd probably already had breakfast. She was comfortable there on her sofa. Why would she want to walk?

"Sure! I was thinking of walking down myself after I finished my coffee. Just like when we were kids, if you get there too late, the best stuff's all gone." She drained the last of her coffee from her mug and smiled brightly. "Let me get my sandals and purse."

In no time, she rejoined him, locking the door behind her. Her glasses were missing, and she'd put on a bra as well as her sandals. The addition failed to help his unruly state of mind, currently pondering which colorful, lacy selection from the laundry line she'd chosen.

Walking alongside Katie again, as they had all those summers ago, was the strangest feeling, as was hearing her voice beside him, so much the same as back then, but richer, and then to glimpse this lovely woman walking by his side out of the corner of his eye, instead of the Katie he'd known.

"Nice morning." Oh, lame, very lame. So much for his talent with words.

"Yes, it is. Supposed to be good and hot today. How was your night last night?"

"Quiet. I planned to read, but my head hit the pillow, and I was out like a light. I slept the night through for the first time in ages, until the mockingbird started his opera routine."

Katie laughed sympathetically. "I have a huge love-hate relationship with those birds, and then there are the sparrows nesting in the maple outside my window. They're always squabbling with each other."

They crossed the two lanes of Route 35 South and passed two more dog walkers.

An elderly man carrying his paper and small bakery sack waved to Katie. "Good morning, Katie."

Katie waved. "Hi, Mr. Blake."

The man looked Matt over with interest.

"Mr. Blake, this is Matt Powell, my old friend from when we were kids. His grandparents owned the house next to mine. Mr. Blake owns the Kitchener's old place."

Matt offered his hand. "Nice to meet you."

"Good to meet you, too. Katie keeps an eye on me and takes care of my cat when I visit my grandkids."

"I love taking care of Simba. He's a sweetie."

"Spoiled rotten, but good company. Well, I won't keep you two. Enjoy your Sunday."

"Have a good day."

At this early hour, the two lanes of Route 35 North were nearly empty of traffic, and they could stroll across without waiting for the light change and then make the turn south.

Lavallette had changed over the decades, yet much remained the same, with no shortage of shops to browse or places to eat. He'd taken a quick cruise around town to get his bearings before arriving at the house. New businesses filled old buildings, old businesses had spiffed up, and new buildings replaced old familiar places.

Dorsey's had a new glossy sign and freshened up their red and white storefront, but inside, the same glass cases waited filled with treats, and the air was fragrant with fresh coffee and welcoming yeasty, sugary scents. Despite the early hour, they had to wait in line.

For newspapers, Matt had his choice of The Star Ledger or The Asbury Park Press. Now, what to eat? Definitely a crumb bun, but Dorsey's still baked the huge, gooey cinnamon rolls remembered. Should he give in to temptation?

~*~

Sweet warmth filled Katie as she watched Matt study the trays of treats, his expression going soft and young as he spotted his favorite cinnamon rolls.

He grinned guiltily. "I'll need to do a few laps of the boardwalk after the sugar high I'll have from all this."

She laughed. "You're on vacation. Live it up."

He nodded and added a cinnamon roll to his crumb bun order. She chose a cinnamon jelly donut and crumb bun for herself and a pecan ring and crusty loaf of rye bread for her parents' visit.

They decided to eat out on the dock. They sat with their legs hanging over edge, sharing the space and lovely morning with the early crabbers and fishermen. The crumb buns made their usual powdered sugar mess over their clothes.

Matt licked the last of the sugar off his fingers and grinned. "That hit the spot. Nice to see some things haven't changed."

"Yep, still the same recipes. I'm so glad they haven't messed with a good thing. Remember Zuccaro's? They tried to change their recipes, go more upscale, oh, ten years ago. Went right out of business. Sad, really, but they never were as good as

Dorsey's."

"I remember your grandpa liked Zuccaro's Kaiser rolls."

Katie laughed. "Right. Grandpa liked they were crisp and crunched when you bit them, but Grandma complained that was only because they were a day old. I think she just didn't like the mess Grandpa made eating them. He never did a good job of cleaning up after his crumbs."

"That's why their dog always sat under his chair."

"Good old Perky, the living vacuum cleaner dog. He made it to seventeen, would you believe?"

"I'm glad. He was a fun dog."

They finished their coffee, checked out the crab catches, and headed on home.

"What are your plans for the day? I need to work a little bit before my folks arrive."

"No plans at all but laziness. Maybe read and walk up to the beach for a swim. I haven't really decided."

"Don't bother buying a beach badge. I have a bunch. You can borrow one while you're here."

"Thanks."

"Please stop in after the beach and say hi when my folks arrive."

"I will. I look forward to seeing them again."

After running in for the promised beach badge, Katie left Matt at the corner of his driveway, her heart light and flipping with a long-forgotten happiness.

She'd just finished tackling some e-mails and was heading out to the shower when her mom called.

"Hey, honey, we're on the Parkway. Traffic's heavy so we'll be a bit, but we'll be there for lunch."

"Okay. I picked up a fresh loaf of rye bread and a tasty surprise for dessert. I have a great second surprise, but that will have to wait for you to see when you get here."

"You cut your hair? New glasses?"

"No, a very nice surprise."

"Now you'll have me wondering the whole way."

"Say hi to Dad. And no, I'm not telling him anything about the surprise either."

After hanging up, she headed outside to take a shower. She'd installed a lovely multi-head shower when she'd renovated the upstairs bathroom last year, but in nice weather, she preferred using the old outside shower stall. There was something perfectly summery about showering with the sun and blue sky above, marigolds bobbing in under the enclosure, the breeze adding cooling chills over her wet skin, and the water splashing onto the pebbles around the wooden platform.

Except today, she felt unusually naked as she stepped under the streaming spray. She'd showered out here all her life, but she'd never experienced this peculiar sensation before. She shook her head. Having Matt next door kept turning all sorts of things topsy-turvy.

After her shower, she headed out to the porch with her laptop to catch up on work until her parents showed up. Her good day continued with two new client inquiries and a paid invoice.

Time flew and her parents arrived.

As she helped them unload groceries, Dad

nodded at Matt's car. "Snazzy car there. How's the new tenant?"

Katie grinned. Matt was still up at the beach, so springing her surprise had to wait.

"Very nice. Quiet so far."

Mom scanned her over. "So what's this surprise you won't tell me about?"

"Still a surprise."

"When are you going to tell us?"

"Oh, sometime between now and supper I think. Not sure. It's not here at the moment."

"This will drive me crazy. You know how much I hate surprises."

Katie kissed her mom. "You adore surprises, and I know you'll completely love this one. You just have to be patient."

Lunch was over, Katie was reading out on the porch and attempting to remain patient while keeping an eye out for Matt's arrival, Mom was knitting, and Dad was drowsing when a knock came at the front porch door.

Nerves buzzing, Katie hopped up. "I'll get it!"

As she opened the door to Matt, an interesting streak of heat rushed through her at the sight of him. He was freshly scrubbed, and his hours up at the beach had added a nice brush of color to his tan.

"Hi, you could have just walked in like always."

"Ah, it's different now that it's your house. We were just kids then, and . . ." He shrugged bashfully.

"Well, come on in. You're still welcome anytime. I've been tormenting Mom and kept you as a surprise."

Happiness bounced in Katie. She caught Matt's hand and tugged him into motion through the porch. This was the best weekend she'd had in forever.

"Hey, Mom, Dad? I've got the surprise."

Puzzlement and happy recognition flashed over her parents' faces as they leapt to the correct conclusion.

Mom sprang to her feet. "Oh, my goodness gracious. Look at you, all grown up. Matt Powell!"

A fresh rush of happiness at Matt's presence filled Katie. "Matt's the tenant next door. Can you believe it?"

Matt offered his hand to Dad. "I thought it'd be fun to visit the old place again."

"Well, how about that. We always wondered how you were doing. You're the spitting image of your dad."

Dad abandoned the handshake and joined Mom in smothering Matt in a hug. Matt hugged them back, sheepish at the fuss.

Dad clapped his shoulder, grinning broadly. "Have a seat, have a seat. Tell us what you've been up to all these years. We were real sorry about your parents splitting up. Sorrier you and your sister were caught in the middle of that trouble."

She caught Matt's tense inhale that conflicted with his casual, confident voice. "It had its rough patches, but Lizzie and I came through fine."

Katie fixed cocktails and brought out the crackers and cheeses to nibble on. She'd prepped plenty of food for supper, and she fully intended to invite Matt to stay.

"Can't get over how much you look like your dad. Knew you in an instant. How are your parents? And your sister?"

After brief, awkward condolences over his parents' passing, the conversation quickly filled with far happier "Remember when" and "Do you remember," and Katie was pleased to see Matt relax.

Mom pulled her aside in the kitchen with a hug. "Oh, Matt's grown up so nice, hasn't he? And he looks at you just like he did when he was a boy and had that sweet crush on you."

Katie rolled her eyes. "Matt didn't have a crush on me. We were simply best friends."

"Honey, he always had the sweetest crush on you. Everyone knew it."

Katie flushed. "Mom! He'll hear you." Matt would be embarrassed, and he definitely didn't have a crush on her then or now. "We're just getting to know each other again. I'm happy just to be friends with him again."

Mom sighed, long, heavy. "Please stop holding what Jeb did to you against other men. Honey, you're too young to be alone like this."

"Mom, I'm perfectly happy. I'm fine. I do not hold Jeb's actions against Matt or anyone else. Honest. Just relax and let Matt and me be friends again. Please?"

Chapter Three

MATT GLADLY ACCEPTED KATIE'S INVITATION to join them for dinner. Despite his original plans for reclusive rest and contemplation, he was also here on a nostalgia trip, so dinner with Katie and her folks fit in perfectly with that goal.

Mr. Vanburen mixed a second round of vodka and tonics for them all. Decades ago, Sunday cocktails for Katie and Matt had been ginger ale and crackers, with Grandpa Vanburen presiding over fixing the grownups' drinks, and Grandma Vanburen hovering between her company and her cooking. Now, Katie hopped up time and again to check on things in the kitchen.

Living here suited Katie. She'd adored staying here for the summer as a child and shared her dreams of living in a house like this when she was grown up.

Matt was passing though her living room from the bathroom to the porch when a troubling realization struck him. He hadn't spotted one single picture of Katie's husband around the house. Katie had always been very sentimental, and she'd been so painfully grieved when she mentioned her loss yesterday, he expected to see at least a few photos mixed in with the pictures of her family scattered around the living room. He scanned around the room. No, none, not even a single wedding picture, nothing.

Katie missed the guy so much she couldn't keep his pictures around? Matt ached for her all over again.

He'd never found someone to love who could love him that much. His last girlfriend, Vivienne, had been the closest to a hard breakup he'd been through. However, in retrospect, he'd loved Vivienne far less thoroughly than he'd believed. He'd gotten over her leaving him too quickly for that to be real love, not even close to a love like Katie had lost.

At least Katie looked to be dealing well with her loss, aside from the troubling picture question. Her stepping into dating again was a good thing, right?

After supper and helping clear the dishes, Matt was about to excuse himself for the night, when Katie's mom snapped the towel.

"Okay, you two, enough waiting on us. It's such a beautiful night. You should go enjoy yourselves. Why don't you take a walk together like you always used to do? Dad and I are going to catch our shows."

Katie turned to him. "I'm game, if you are?"

"Sure. A walk would be a good idea after all that food. I really enjoyed the meal. Thanks again."

"You're welcome. Okay, let me grab my purse in case we decide to stop for ice cream or something while we're out. We used to do that too."

Up at the boardwalk, they enjoyed the view of a hot orange sunset to the west and the approaching cool dark of night to the east. Warmth still radiated from the boards after the long day baking under the sun.

"Your parents are looking great. Really good to see them again. Still as nice as I remembered them to be."

He released a long, tense breath. "Being back here is the strangest feeling, a mix of being in a place I don't know and of having never left—And of coming home. Very peculiar, considering I was only here for a few summers."

"I can only imagine." She gave his hand a brief squeeze and let go. "Oh! You know what? They have live music at the Seaward Inn tonight. This guy plays piano and sings. He's very talented and funny. Would you like to stop in there and check him out?"

"We can give it a try."

More nostalgia rose. How Pop had loved the lunch and early bird specials at the Seaward Inn.

They crossed at the light and walked three blocks north. Shops lined the street and vehicles filled the diagonal parking spots as far up and down the street as he could see.

One dark shop caught Matt's eye out of all the shops open late to lure in tourists. A faded and dusty For Sale sign leaned in the picture window. If he remembered correctly, the building had once been a small bungalow home. No telling what business had recently occupied the stripped-bare space.

The exterior of the Seaward Inn had undergone some remodeling since he'd been here last, but still had the old broad front porch. The original structure had been built as a hotel around 1910, and had endured some good, bad, and interesting renovations over the century. He remembered an oddly sloping floor in part of the dining area that must have once been a side porch.

The place was busy, but luck was in their favor, and the hostess found them a small table for two in the lounge near the piano.

As Katie studied the selections on the drinks menu, her brow wrinkled in a puzzled frown.

"See what you'd like to order?"

"I'm not sure. Normally, I prefer wine or a vodka and tonic, but tonight seems to call for something special. Something celebratory."

She looked up, and her happy smile rammed him with a serious, body-tightening jolt of desire. The low light of the lounge deepened her eyes, accentuating the soft curves of her face and a mouth perfect for kissing.

Damn, he'd never get used to this desire for Katie, no matter how intriguing or tempting or gorgeous she was. Lusting after a childhood friend was just so . . .

Matt wrenched his mind around to study Katie as if they'd just met. Which, considering a gap of twenty years, was a reasonable exercise. They might know each other's childhood likes and dreams, but he knew far too little about this grown-up and gorgeous Katie, a business owner, a woman who'd loved, wed, and been widowed. She was his Katie, and yet, not his Katie.

"How about you, have you decided?"

Decided? Yes, that there might be some truth to the old adage you can't go home again. If she was any other woman he'd met, pursuing this attraction would be an effortless decision.

But she was *Katie*.

~*~

Matt was staring at her as if she was one of the menu selections—and Katie had an overwhelming craving to be tasted.

"Matt?"

He stretched back in his chair, tensely raking a hand through his hair. "Since we had those vodka and tonics earlier, I think I'll keep it simple and stick to a vodka martini with a twist."

Katie refocused, scanning the usual list of summery drinks: margaritas, piña coladas, daiquiris, and mojitos. They had a long list of fancy martinis, many quite strange in their ingredients and far too sugary. The lavender martini caught her eye. That qualified as different, and the description sounded tasty and light.

"I know. I'll try the lavender martini."

Matt grinned. "Sounds interesting. Do you want any food to nibble on with the drink?"

At his words, an utterly inappropriate picture of her nibbling on Matt's firm mouth blared into her brain. Heat rushed through her. Oh, no, oh, no, where on earth had that come from? Well, it had been so long since she'd nibbled or done anything else with a man and sitting across from Matt in a restaurant was so much like a date. Matt was handsome and fun, but this crazy urge to nibble on him and more? Totally needed to go away.

"I'm still full from supper, but thanks."

Their drinks arrived, offering a welcome distraction from her unruly imagination. The martini was a lovely color, scented with the lavender and lemon, and rimmed with pastel lavender sugar. Her first sip confirmed she'd chosen well. Light and refreshing, the drink was nicely balanced between tart and sweet.

Matt raised a brow. "What do you think?"

"Delicious."

Going out proved to be a great idea. The pianist was entertaining, and the music made the pauses in their conversation pass by easily, but the moments of silence between them were comfortably free of the strain to fill time with words. This quiet between them far more resembled the peace of their childhood friendship when they once spent hours together fishing, reading, writing, drawing, or crabbing.

To her surprise, during one song when the pianist encouraged everyone to join in and sing "Brown Eyed Girl," Matt did, in a low, smooth baritone, his intense gaze locked on her as if he meant the words for her.

Since they were enjoying the music and in no rush to leave, they both ordered a second drink. Between songs, conversation flowed easily around safe and simple subjects like television shows, movies, and books they'd read. They lost track of time, and the pianist's finale and goodnight caught them by surprise.

Matt pushed aside his empty glass. "Would you like anything else or would you like to go?"

She laughed. "Oh, no, I couldn't handle another drink. We can head out if you like."

Between the before-supper cocktails hours ago, however light, and these two drinks, she was left relaxed and pleasantly giddy. A third would leave her in a snoozing ball in her seat.

"It's a good thing I don't have to head off to work in the morning. Well, I mean, go anywhere to work. Since my office is my house. But those stairs, you know." She winced at her silliness.

Matt just chuckled and raised his hand for the check.

Once they stepped outside, and the warm humid night wrapped around her, Katie found she was giddier than she first thought, bubbling with happiness and the urge to pull Matt to her and—

Whoa there! Note to self: you're definitely a one-martini girl.

They walked up to the corner and paused to wait for the light change. The heavy northbound traffic crawled by as weekenders headed home late for ordinary life and work in the morning.

Steadier now, Katie inhaled deeply, savoring the steamy night and the ease washing through her. She loved the smells of the shore: a blend of salt, brine, and seaweed, someone's roses in the garden, food odors from the restaurants, a whiff of coconut as another couple passed them. Then there was Matt's own warm scent, contributing a heartfelt tension to her comfortable relaxation.

"This has been the best day. Thank you." Without thinking, she caught his hand, abruptly reluctant to head home and end this evening. "Do you still want to walk the boardwalk before we head back? I'm up for a walk if you are."

~*~

"Sure." Matt was in no hurry for the evening to end.

An interesting mix of memories and the present washed through him as they strolled up the block to the boardwalk. He and Katie had walked hand in hand on occasion all those years ago, but this was tremendously, pleasurably different.

Scattered lights glowed in houses and televisions flickered. People sat on their porches, enjoying the breath of breeze cooling the steamy, salty night air. A lighter flared as someone stepped onto the front steps for a smoke. Stars twinkled above. The endless, roaring rush and roll of waves breaking on the beach erased the drone of traffic. Moonlight brushed the dark ocean with silver, and faint lights glinted on the horizon.

"Short end or long end or we could walk down on the beach?"

He glanced north and south along the long wooden boardwalk. The evening was late enough that only a scattering of people shared the peaceful stretch. "Either way you like."

"Oh, long end tonight. That will give my head a chance to clear. I shouldn't have had that second drink, but we were having such a good time and in no hurry, and the first was so delicious."

"You're okay?" He had to admit he was feeling his second drink, and he was glad they were walking rather than driving. However, he was relaxed, and he enjoyed the fit of her warm, soft hand in his and this freedom from time constraints.

"I'm fine. No worries." She smiled and gave his hand a light squeeze.

They walked on, passing other people out enjoying a late night walk, chatting and laughing together over childhood memories long buried by time and daily life. Lamps and flickering televisions allowed glimpses inside the houses they passed.

After strolling several blocks, they paused at one of the covered wood pavilions and walked to the edge of the stairs leading down between the dunes to the beach. A shimmering full moon and starry sky added a dreamy shimmer to the night. Below on the deserted beach, a couple wandered along the water line, sidestepping the endless tide washing the sand. Out on the dark ocean, pinpricks of light steadily cruised northward, maybe a cruise ship or a cargo ship.

Katie leaned against the railing and tipped her face to him with that dimpled smile, so familiar and so new. The soft light of the full moon highlighted her dark eyes, soft lips, the alluring curve of her cleavage, and smooth cling of her dress to her hips.

Twenty years ago, he'd liked Katie with his whole heart, but that had been a safe, clueless, and innocent liking. Nana might have called it puppy love. Now? The old like was still there, strong as always, plus something different, deeper, and far from innocent.

He was no longer eight or thirteen. They weren't best friends anymore. What they were now? Hell, he was clueless. Familiar strangers? What he did have a clue about was how the tempting curve of her soft lips and that familiar dimple called to be kissed.

Maybe the feeling was just the vodka talking.

Or maybe not.

Why couldn't he want Katie? They were both adults, single, and unattached. Why not give in to what he wanted for once in his life? What could one kiss do?

Worse case, acting on the crazy idea had to clean thinking of her as anything but an old friend out of his system. He was likely over-thinking everything, a habitual problem of his. However, he preferred prudent consideration of decisions, and decisive action once deliberation was concluded.

A kiss would cure him, maybe, or at least give him a hint one way or another as to whether she could feel the same. At the moment, he had little hope this consuming attraction was leaving his system anytime soon.

But, what if you botch this? What if you screw up the friendship? Best friends forever?

Too late. He'd screwed up their friendship years ago when he abandoned staying in touch with Katie. Teenage moods, to be sure, and his childish anger and hurt were no fault of Katie's, but he'd turned his back on her and the happiness he'd treasured in their friendship all the same. He'd just have to be careful and do a better job this time around.

Please, let me get this right. He lowered his head and touched his mouth to hers, cupping her face in his hands, and yielded wholly into the reality of desiring Katie.

Her lips were soft and warm, and she tasted of sweet lavender and lemon. His heart panged at her sharp shocked intake of breath, but he brushed his mouth over hers, keeping his hands gently cradling her face, resisting the urge to let them explore her further and clinging to thinning patience as he endeavored to convey both the deep desire and the tenderness he felt for her. Would she pull away or not?

Katie shivered and stilled, but, instead of taking the escape his light touch offered, remained quiet in his grasp.

Encouraged, he grazed his lips over to taste her dimple, sliding his fingers into the wavy silk of her hair. Returning to her mouth, he nipped gently at her lush lower lip, coaxing, savoring this moment, the endless wash and rumble of the ocean, and the warm, dark embrace of night making the shadowy pavilion private and personal.

Only, she remained quietly passive under his kisses. Uninterested or unready?

Saddened, he pressed a lingering kiss to her lips, prepared to step back, apologize, and blame the drinks, when Katie softened with a shivering rush of breath, wrapped her arms around his neck, and lifted herself into their kiss.

Thank you!

On a surge of heady joy, he caressed his mouth over hers, curbing the hunger for more than these slow, intimate explorations. Even if these were the only kisses they ever shared, he'd never regret taking the chance of moving beyond old friends. Kissing Katie was beyond any kiss he'd imagined.

Kissing Katie was better.

Still trading brushes and gentle bites, he slid his hands over her, letting them come to rest on her hips.

On a dreamy sigh, she opened her mouth to his

in sweet, eager abandon. He sank into the deep kiss, filled with fierce elation, as if he'd finally come home to the place he'd always belonged.

Chapter Four

SHOCK, AMAZEMENT, AND DESIRE RICOCHETED through Katie. Matt's hot mouth on hers, his lips, his tongue . . . They were kissing as if their lives depended on never parting. Soaring on the crazy, intense pleasure, she was gripping him with desperation, body to body.

The need for such intimate contact warred with the knowledge of exactly who was kissing her, but even her ongoing shock failed to force her to push him away. She craved every moment of this uninhibited kiss.

How she *needed*. The heat of desire licking through her shook her to the core. She'd made mistakes out of need before and now . . . Matt. She was far from ready for this to happen with anyone, let alone Matt.

Only, this didn't feel like a mistake. Contrarily,

she hungered for more.

A sigh, hers. A groan, his. His hands sliding over her bottom, gripping her close. Her hands . . . her hands now gripping his hips, needing him closer, pulling him closer.

"Awesome. Go for it, dude." A passerby laughed and loped past down the stairs.

New shock rattled her. "Oh!"

They were kissing on the boardwalk, in public, in front of *people*.

Matt smiled against her mouth, staying in the kiss.

However, for her, the moment's magic was broken. She was far too startled and too aware where they were. She leaned away, blinking up at him, and pressed a hand to his chest.

Heat filled Matt's dark eyes, and his face was grave. "I won't say I'm sorry."

Speechless, she nodded, unsure if she wanted him to be sorry or if she wanted him to ignore her halt and give her more kisses.

"I'll walk you home."

They walked in silence. The warm humid night clung close, keeping the need for Matt's arms to wrap her close simmering. Katie's emotions swung madly between the urge to discuss the kiss and the sense the kiss had said more than either of them expected. Blaming the two drinks or the full moon would be cowardly. Yes, their kissing was a mistake, but feeling guilty for enjoying his kisses was ridiculous.

She was free to be kissed. Matt had kissed her. She'd enjoyed his kisses. End of story.

They stopped at the end of her driveway, the

silence between them huge and awkward, and he faced her, his expression worried.

That worry—that was a problem. She had to assure Matt she wasn't upset with him. They shouldn't have kissed, but if she had to make a mistake, at least their kiss had been a lovely, memorable mistake.

"The kiss. It was okay . . . I mean, that you kissed me was okay, not that the kiss was just okay." Oh, she was babbling. "Ah . . . We shouldn't have, maybe, but I'm not upset with you." She lifted on her toes and kissed his cheek. "I'll see you tomorrow. Okay?"

A lopsided smile replaced his rumpled worried face. "I'd like that."

Only, the brief goodnight kiss he pressed to her mouth felt more like a challenge than acceptance.

"Goodnight." She turned and scooted for the front door, kicking herself the whole way for being a babbling ditz.

Mom was awake, reading on the porch. Through an open window, Katie glimpsed Dad stretched out asleep on the living room sofa, softly snoring through a home renovation program.

"Hey, Katie sweetie. You were out late. Have fun?" Mom set aside her book, smiling expectantly.

"Matt and I ended up going to the Seaward Inn for a drink. The music was great, and then we, ah, walked the long end of the boardwalk."

"I'm glad you had a fun time together. It was such a delightful surprise seeing Matt all grown up. He's matured into a very nice, charming man."

A steamy flush rushed over Katie. "Yes, he has."

More surprises than Mom might guess.

Charming was true, but nice was far too bland a description after experiencing his kisses. How about astounding, talented, and overwhelming?

"I hope you two can spend more time together while he's here."

"I think we will. I hope so."

Finding she honestly did wish to see him, despite the flares of anxiety, was a heady surprise.

"I think I'm going to call it a night and read in bed for a bit."

"Sleep tight, Katie. Love you."

"Love you too, Mom." She kissed her mom with a quick hug and headed upstairs.

Shut in the refuge of the bathroom, she pressed a cold, wet washcloth to her face.

Oh, she'd definitely made a mistake drinking that second martini. She must have given Matt the totally wrong idea, but it had been too long since she'd simply relaxed and had fun like that. None of her recent forays into dating had progressed beyond a friendly thanks-for-a good-evening kiss to the cheek. Matt's kiss, well that had been a wonderful kiss. She hadn't been kissed like that, well, since ever.

No, since Jeb. She really needed to learn to let herself remember the happy times with Jeb. There had been many perfect kisses shared with Jeb, many lovely times. However, these days, separating out the happy from the hurtful still escaped her.

Maybe she was just blowing the evening all out of proportion. They'd shared a kiss. Just a spontaneous moment instigated by vodka, a warm summer night, and the inherent romance of a quiet moonlit stroll on the boardwalk with a charming man. Anyone would cave to such delightful circumstances.

Be realistic, Katie. You're in no way ready for a new man in your life romantically.

Sadly, true. She needed more time before she'd be ready for a relationship again.

But . . . what if Matt thought she was some flighty, kissing anyone kind of person? Had she given the impression she expected more from him than enjoying his friendship again? She struggled to remember how she'd behaved in the restaurant. Normal, she'd thought. They'd talked, enjoyed the music.

He'd kissed her. On purpose, deliberately, like a date, like a lover who desired her. Undeniably, positively not a kiss to dismiss as an accident.

Katie groaned. No denying she'd kissed him back, enjoyed kissing him, and had plastered herself against him like she'd wanted more than kisses from him.

What on earth would she do tomorrow when she saw him?

She flopped onto her bed and stared at the ceiling. She'd made a mistake thinking Matt was the boy she knew from years ago. Not a boy, not anymore by a long shot. She still felt the soft strength of his mouth on hers. They weren't thirteen-year-old BFF's anymore, however much she wanted to cling to those happy innocent memories.

Tomorrow, she simply needed to explain she hadn't meant to give him the wrong idea about her intentions. They really couldn't do that again, however lovely a moment, however lovely a kiss.

Adoring Matt as a friend years ago was merely

being mistakenly reinterpreted by her current adult self as a romantic interest. This need was only a yearning for the connection she'd lost with Jeb and was currently missing in her life. She wasn't looking for a romantic relationship, and anyhow, he was only here for two weeks, and then he'd return to his own busy life.

Now that she'd found Matt again, she didn't want to lose his friendship. She needed friendship more than she needed a lover.

Oh, tomorrow promised to be awkward. She brushed a finger over her lips.

However, someday, when she was ready to love again . . . she absolutely wanted kisses like Matt's.

~*~

The next day, a knock at his porch door interrupted Matt's quiet morning of reading.

He found Katie, beach bag in hand, smiling as if nothing had changed between them since yesterday morning. She wore a white cover-up, her hair was tucked into a neat braid under her floppy sun hat, and daisies decorated her sandals.

"Hey, Katie. Come on in. Been up to the beach?" He opened the door for her.

"No, I'm heading there now. Mom and Dad left for home after breakfast, and since I finished my to-do list for the morning, I thought I'd treat myself to lazing on the beach for a few hours. It's a gorgeous day, far too nice to waste staying inside glued to my computer, and I was wondering if you'd like to join me."

This was his old Katie, open, expectant, enthusiastic. How could he say no?

Patience, he cautioned himself, take things

slowly. No diving in like last night.

"I'd like that very much."

Depression slunk in as he readied for the beach and met her out on the porch. Why was he even trying? She was right. An awesome kiss, but they shouldn't have. This short, peaceful respite was deceptive. He should be satisfied with being friends again.

Damn it, reality sucked. In eleven days, he'd be gone. In eleven days, he'd have the partnership he'd been busting his ass for all these years, before his goal age, and he'd have no time for resting on his laurels. His real life held no room for a patient courtship. All too soon, he'd be busting his ass again, proving himself all over again and reaching for that next rung on the success ladder. His real life was research, prep, court, depositions, meetings, and phone calls, working seven days a week, rising in the dark a.m., and bringing his caseload home at night. Being a partner might shift some of the tasks and responsibilities off his back, but none of the pressure. A whole new barrel of pressures and duties accompanied the prestige. They wanted him because he was an ass-buster, a go-getter. He wanted them because they were a prime stepping-stone to his further career goals.

Up at the beach, they studied the bright stretch of sand crowded with families and umbrellas. He'd checked earlier, and the tide was going low. They walked south along the beach until they found an uncrowded spot to spread their towels and settle their bags, water bottles, and reading material.

Katie slipped off her cover-up, revealing a skimpy purple bikini splashed with white flowers.

She turned, every curve displayed for him, beautifully filling in all his imagination had speculated at, and held out a bottle of sunscreen.

"Could you do my back? I always miss a spot or two. I really should get the spray kind." She swept her braid aside and offered her back to him.

He froze. It was just her back. What was the big deal? They'd done each other's backs twenty years ago.

However, twenty years made an immense difference in the details, his attention, and his reaction. Twenty years ago, he'd been dumb as a rock about girls, and Katie didn't have these luscious curves.

Thin strings fastened the bikini top at her nape and below the fine lines of her shoulder blades. He set his jaw and obediently drizzled the lotion over her shoulders and back. He just needed to be brisk, businesslike—

Katie giggled. "That tickles."

Why, oh, why couldn't she have a spray bottle? He shifted painfully, thankful he'd worn his baggiest swim trunks.

Matt set the bottle aside on the towel, and took a steadying breath. In for penny, in for a pound. He tentatively dragged his fingertips through the creamy lotion, immediately failing at the brisk, businesslike approach the moment he registered the sensual slip of his palms over her soft, warm skin.

"Ooh, that feels lovely. Thanks." She sighed, and the shivering release of tension in the muscles under his hand sent his imagination whirling how she might shiver in an entirely different sort of release.

His conflict worsened as he glided his hands lower and lower, learning the curves of her waist and hips, and his hands actually shook as he brushed past the gentle indent of her bottom.

Done, done, done. He fell back a step, dying with desire.

She turned, smiling innocently. "Would you like me to do you now?"

Yes!

No, no, oh, no way. "No, thanks. I'm good. Took care of it back at the house while I changed." Thank goodness, he had. His body's intense, rigid attention was already embarrassing enough. He wasn't eighteen, damn it. Having her hands on him would be a huge mistake right now. Pure disaster.

"Okay. If you need more, just ask." She scooped up the sunscreen and ran a streak of the cream over her chest.

He swallowed hard. Oh, did he need more. More touch . . .

More space.

"I'm going to check out the water." He kicked off his sandals and fled for the water.

"Enjoy!"

Escaping failed to help the situation as his stubborn imagination vividly elaborated on how continuing the sunscreen application over the delicate skin of Katie's breasts and abdomen would look and feel. And layering in sensations of their boardwalk kiss . . .

Matt groaned and dropped into the shallow, warm ocean water that needed to be thirty degrees colder.

He wasn't here to kindle a romance. He was

here to clear his head and carefully select the next rung in his career ladder. He stared at the open horizon and focused his thoughts onto the excellent offers, and the very different cities the jobs would take him to.

Only, he didn't care.

This apathy was a problem. If only one firm stood out from the others. He could choose by throwing a dart with eyes shut. All were exceptional firms, offering terrific financial packages, new challenges, and most importantly, prime positioning for his future career advancement. Anyone else would have jumped without a second thought and taken anyone of them. What more did he want?

His lack of an answer was a real problem. He was too young to be having a midlife existential crisis.

He still had eleven days left for making his decision.

He glanced over to Katie lying face up and at ease on her towel.

Why are you pondering answerless questions you don't give a crap about today when you can enjoy this view?

Damn it, he was doing it again. However, shutting his eyes failed to erase the tempting picture. That was his Katie virtually naked over there but for the tiny strings and meager triangles of fabric covering her shapely breasts and the equally skimpy stretch of her bikini bottoms. Imagining her completely naked was an easy, logical leap and a hell of a lot more interesting than his current existential crisis.

Hell, time for the truth. He didn't want to be just

friends. They hadn't been friends for twenty years. They weren't thirteen anymore. They weren't good old pals. He was fooling himself if he believed he could settle for what they'd had as children.

Yes, of course, he wanted their old, comfortable, happy connection, but he also wanted *more*. Innocent walks, chatting over donuts, bike rides, or reading on the porch would never satisfy the craving unleashed last night by their kiss. He'd moved far beyond the simple desires he'd had at thirteen or ten or eight. The woman drowsing in the sun was no longer his tomboy-dreamer best friend in the world, and he was damn glad she wasn't.

What next? Katie had said they shouldn't have kissed, but her body language had spoken reams during that kiss. Years of reading people in legal arenas had taught him to look beneath the cover of words for the truth in their actions and reactions. Only, this wasn't a trial, and despite his time constraints, he couldn't barrel in on the point. He needed to be respectful of her grief and love for her husband. He'd just have to use the finesse he'd honed in obtaining the truth out of witnesses to persuade Katie to admit the truth of her own desires.

So, time for a plan.

Step one: Stop denying his feelings.

Step two: Acknowledge that Katie, now known as Katherine Elizabeth Vanburen-MacBain, was gorgeous and sexy.

Step three: Acknowledge that his wanting the said gorgeous, sexy Katherine Elizabeth Vanburen-MacBain in his bed was a healthy, normal, *adult* response.

Step four: Act on that desire for Katie. For just once in his life, wasn't it time he did something he wanted rather than restrain himself to what was expected? The time had come to learn what he wanted beyond that corner office and another stepping-stone to his future successes.

He grinned. Doing something about his feelings for Katie promised to be a fascinating challenge.

~*~

Katie was glad to see Matt's swim had washed away his dour mood and left him relaxed. He did have a lot on his mind. Deciding on a job was never easy, and adding in the upcoming major cross-country move, well, his tension was understandable.

Between cooling swims, they lazed under the baking sun, read, and napped, until hunger finally drove them to head home.

She wriggled against the drying salt prickling over her skin and sand making itself known in uncomfortable places. "I love, love the beach, but, ugh, how did we put up with being sticky, salty, and sandy all day long? I so want a shower right now."

Matt laughed. "Mom was always baffled how we could rinse off, take a thorough bath, and still have sand stuck everywhere."

They reached 35 North. Matt glanced up the street. "How about some ice cream on the walk home? Is that shop Sprinkles and Jimmies any good?"

She groaned. "You're a terrible influence on my diet, you know. Their ice cream is delicious and I'd love some."

"We'll eat a disgustingly healthy supper to

make up for it."

Matt's grin reminded her of Jeb's smile when he was cooking up some off the wall activity. However, Matt wasn't Jeb, so she must be reading him entirely wrong.

They both chose the handmade sugar cones, she went with her usual strawberry and vanilla, and Matt decided on the Dutch chocolate and vanilla swirl.

As they continued their walk homeward, she kept sneaking peeks at Matt. Their day in the sun left him with a glow of color, sand grains clung here and there to his arms, chest, and legs, and his hair had dried in messy, salty curls. A small part of her kept expecting to see Matt of twenty years ago. A wild and crazy part of her was totally hungering for something far more satisfying than the rich, creamy ice cream and completely intrigued at finding this handsome, deep-voiced other Matt in place of her fond memory. Seeing him in swim trunks, his broad, muscular, bare chest swirled with dark hair on view all day had to be partly to blame.

As for asking him to apply sunscreen to her back—that had been a lovely, terrible mistake.

Oh, it had been far too long since she'd had a man's hands on her bare skin. Despite her anger with Jeb, she missed his hands on her and the press of his body. Matt's smoothing lotion over her back had ignited a relentless craving for more touch, more *everything*. More was entirely dangerous and foolish.

Just watching him lick and bite his ice cream — oh, holy cow, her mind was spinning that ordinary act into amazing, tempting directions, thinking of him licking and biting . . .

At her fresh, steamy flush, Katie swallowed tensely, unsettled by the sizzling twist of desire.

"Your ice cream's dripping. Catch it!"

She jolted and chased the pink slide over her fingers and down her wrist, tasting ocean salt, strawberry, and vanilla, laughing as she had to race to lick away more messy drips.

Matt's hand closed around her wrist. As she looked up, he drew her hand toward him and leisurely licked her fingers clean.

She froze, stunned at the sensuous, warm slide of his tongue.

Eyes twinkling with mischief, he stole a bite of her ice cream and grinned, and then licked his own dripping ice cream.

Her mind unhelpfully transposed his slow lick to the sensation of his tongue on her fingers, and shivering heat swept her again.

A shower was definitely in order. A cold one, oh, boy.

The race to eat their rapidly melting ice creams evolved into silliness, and they were both laughing and sticky by the time they dropped their bags and towels on her porch steps and ate the last soggy remains of the cones.

Finished, Katie pushed to her feet, feeling silly and absurdly nervous, holding her sticky hand helplessly in the air. She couldn't exactly tell him to go home. "I, ah, really need to shower off before I go inside."

Matt nodded, his smile growing. "Okay."

"So . . . ah, make yourself at home. The key's in the side pocket of my bag. I'll be just a minute."

"Sure."

She grabbed a clean towel off the line and dashed a beeline for the outdoor shower. She hung her towel and cover-up on the hook and turned to shut the door—

Only to collide with Matt, who steadied her with an arm around her waist, shut the door for her, and flipped the latch.

She blinked at him. "Oh—" The roomy enclosure suddenly felt tight.

"Figured we might as well conserve water and rinse off together." His passionate and determined gaze clashed with his playful tone.

Say something.

"We can't shower together!" she squeaked.

Releasing her, he turned the taps. "Sure we can."

Hot water gushed and sprayed between them on the wooden plank platform. After adjusting the temperature, he stepped under the shower and tipped his face to the rushing water, scrubbing his hands over his head.

She was still frozen in astonishment when he caught an arm around her and tugged her under the spray. She sputtered, laughed, and swiped at the streaming water over her face.

"Matt!"

"Feels good, doesn't it?"

She wiped at her face again. "Yes, it does, but—"

Matt splayed his hands over her bottom, drawing her closer. "Isn't that enough? Just letting things feel good?"

"But—" She caught her hands onto his biceps.

"Just relax."

Relax? With Matt's hands on her butt? With her breasts crushed against his bare chest? With his rigid, unmistakable erection jutting against her belly?

He caressed her back. "Just relax and enjoy. All we're doing is rinsing off." His voice lowered into a sensual rumble as he nudged her around. "Just shut your eyes and unwind."

He ran his hands up to her shoulders and rubbed his thumbs into her tense muscles, working in toward her spine and then to the base of her neck.

Oh, so good. She surrendered with a heartfelt groan of pleasure.

His chuckle rumbled behind her, and he massaged her neck and the tight muscles at the base of her skull and behind her ears. The tension and silly panic flowed from her with the streaming warm water and the sun shining on them. Then, he was unraveling her braid, and the soft tropical scent of her shampoo filled the air. He worked the suds through her hair, and she surrendered to being pure putty in his hands, standing dreamily under the massage of water and his strong fingers rubbing and kneading over her scalp.

After thoroughly rinsing her hair, Matt shifted around to face her and cupped her face.

Caught in the blissful surrender, she tipped her face to his, wanting the coming kiss, and caught her hands on his hips, drawing close as his mouth came down on hers in a slow, lazy kiss. As if she were an ice cream melting under the massaging cascade of water, he indulged in leisurely bites and licks. Their bodies brushed together, wet, warm, and slick, his arousal hard beneath his swim trunks. The crazy need to wrap herself around him consumed her, and she groaned.

His kiss lightened, sweetened. "Katie . . ."

His rough voice, dark eyes, and long potent pause sent her insides clenching with need. Whatever he was about to ask, she was so afraid her answer was yes.

Surprisingly, he pulled away, clearing his throat. "I, uh—don't know how you condition your hair, or . . . My sister always does my niece's hair up in a twist and lets the conditioner soak in."

The spell broke, sensibility returned, and she could breathe again. "Ah, right, yes. I do something like that also.

Saved. Or not?

Chapter Five

MATT DRAGGED IN A STEADYING BREATH AND peeled his hands from Katie's hips. Time to give them both a break, before he did something neither was ready for.

Katie shivered and grabbed her towel to her. "I—I'll do that when I shower up properly. The, uh, conditioner. I'll head inside and change. Then we can have a drink and start supper."

"Sounds good. I'll wash up here and be right with you."

He let Katie escape. After latching the door, he stripped to rinse away the last of the sand from his swim trunks and his body. Damned stuff got *everywhere*.

Well, his impulsively joining her in the shower was either a raging success or a real bad move. Hell, both. A raging success, because he'd proved the desire he'd felt in her last night during their boardwalk kiss was more than a residual effect of her lavender martinis. Most definitely a bad move, because he was miserably hard, and he wanted her more than ever.

He'd slipped in after her in play, meaning to keep whatever happened light and fun, like spontaneously licking the ice cream from her fingers. Only, the pleasure in massaging her shoulders had been like striking a match. He'd wanted to get his hands in her hair, on her . . . everywhere, and resisting taking a kiss had been futile.

Frustrated and aching, he wrapped his hand around himself, shuddering, and shut his eyes, wishing his grip was Katie's touch, Katie's hand, Katie's mouth. That visual knocked him fast and hard over the edge. He came, short, intense, and deeply unsatisfactory, but a relief all the same. He caught his breath, grabbed the soap, and finished scrubbing, fighting to clear his head.

Backing off wasn't an option, but he had better watch himself and use his brain here. He wanted Katie, to an insane degree, but he also wanted to avoid hurting her by foolhardiness. This was rapidly becoming far more important than curiosity and needing a distraction from career decisions. He wanted this connection between them to be more than getting into her bed and scoring some vacation sex. If they were moving into a relationship beyond simple friendship, he wanted a relationship with a future.

And there remained the troubling matter of her dead husband's hold on her heart. Could she hold any room in there for him beyond the tenuous link of childhood friendship?

Ah, you're forgetting you're leaving for good in eleven days. Remember? Inconvenient for building a relationship deeper than a casual fling.

Stop. He'd figure out all the details. He hadn't reached this rung in his career by caving to niggling doubts. There were always answers, always ways to negotiate a mutually satisfying conclusion.

He turned off the taps, wrung out his trunks, and pulled them back on. He headed into the house.

"Katie?" He walked into her kitchen.

Listening, he caught the steady murmur of running water upstairs. His unruly mind merrily envisioned her again under the streaming shower, this time without the flowery purple bikini.

He groaned and pulled out two glasses to fix drinks. Maybe some snacks would be good as well to carry them over until they decided what to make for supper. After perusing the contents of her fridge, he threw together a tray of crackers, cheeses, and grapes.

First off, he had to persuade Katie they could have an excellent relationship together. Imagining her being with him, well, that made even a D.C. winter something to look forward to. He sank onto the porch couch and sipped at his drink.

However, if this thing sparking between them did work out, what about Katie's work? In theory, since she had a home-based career, and all her clientele was online, packing up and relocating without disruption to her business should be nearly painless. He'd have to revise his house hunt plans and budget from a low-maintenance condo to something larger, homier, and near the water, if possible, as well as calculate in ways to let her keep her house here for vacations . . .

The muffled ring of his phone rang startled him from his musing. He dug the phone out from his bag. The caller was his real estate agent Vera in Seattle, so he answered.

"Hello, Vera. Good to hear from you. Do you have good news for me today?"

"I have very good news, Matt. The buyers accepted your counteroffer, with only one additional request. In addition to the items already included in the listing, they want you to include the living room and dining room furniture."

Asking for the furniture was a ballsy negotiation move on the buyers' part, the value of which easily exceeded their concession on the purchase price by double. Did he really want buyers who were likely to nitpick every step of the way through closing?

Katie joined him on the porch, her hair damp and loose, and smile anxious.

His heart took a happy little jump that was for more than how sweetly sexy she looked despite the baggy T-shirt and knit shorts hiding her curves. She settled into the chair opposite him with the drink waiting for her, but he half-expected that distance after their experience together in the shower.

As Matt studied Katie, a fresh tumult of emotions filled him. Deciding on the new offer took him all of two seconds.

"Tell them I'll list what pieces I'm specifically willing to include, and if they agree to the itemized list, then we have a deal. I'll e-mail the list to you first thing tomorrow morning." Less furniture to move and he only cared about a few of the smaller pieces anyhow.

"Great. I'll look for your e-mail." Vera ended the call.

Matt turned the volume down to vibrate and tucked the phone away in his bag.

Katie's thought expression warmed into a smile. "You're grinning, so good news I'm assuming?"

Good news, true, but far from the genuine reason for his smile.

"That was my real estate agent with an update. I just accepted an offer on my house."

"Congratulations." She raised her glass. "Thanks for fixing the drinks and snacks."

"No problem." He tapped his glass to hers. "Now, you and I need to discuss something important."

Embarrassment flashed over her face and her eyes widened.

Damn, Katie really wasn't ready for any of this, was she? She needed time, but he had little leeway on that to give her.

"Supper. I'm starving. What do you want to eat for supper?"

Her laugh rang out, and the tension between them eased. He kept his hands to himself, giving her the space she seemed to need through the takeout pizza and salad and watching television.

The tactic worked, and he enjoyed seeing her relax. However, when he called it a night, he was determined to make her remember how good their kisses were. Let her think about their kisses tonight and tomorrow while she was working and they were apart.

Cupping her cheek, he studied the anxiety and

desire mixing in her wide eyes, wanting to erase her worries. He'd take just one kiss. No asking for more.

"Matt—"

He touched his mouth to hers.

Contenting himself to explore the curves of her lips, he slipped his fingers through her hair to cradle her head in his hands and eased into a slow, long kiss.

With a torn groan, Katie joined wholeheartedly into the kiss. Restrained hunger seared into hot, shaking his good intentions.

His pulse racing, he dropped his hands away. "I'll see you tomorrow afternoon at three o'clock. Sleep well."

~*~

Sleep well? If only.

After a night of tossing and turning between half-remembered, confusing dreams of Jeb and Matt, Katie made a pot of coffee and ordered herself to put Matt and his kisses out of her mind if she hoped to be productive. Today had to be a workday, no matter how the little Katie in her begged for a play day knowing Matt was next door. She had images to search for, invoices to send, e-mail inbox to empty, a header to redesign, two blog posts to schedule, and a new client website to build. After yesterday's kisses, they probably could use a cooling-off break.

What was he doing this morning? The forecast for scattered thunderstorms made the day iffy for the beach.

Stop. Focus on work.

The time and work flew by, the coffee pot emptied, she reached inbox zero, found a nice selection of images for a few of her projects, and played with the header job until she'd tweaked that project to where she wanted. She was digging into a new website design when the first thunderstorm rolled in.

The storm was a doozy, all flash and crash, and the rain fell in torrents. Luckily, the power stayed on and she was able to keep working. She wanted to get this draft complete and ready for her client's review. She felt she'd nailed the design concept and colors, but clients could be fickle even when they provided clear-cut ideas in the beginning.

The thunderstorm slackened into spits and spatters, and the sun broke through the overcast.

A knock at her front door stirred her attention away from the monitor, followed by Matt's "Hey, Katie? Got a minute?"

"Come on in."

Ignoring the leap of happiness at his early arrival, she saved her work and pushed her chair away from the desk. She slipped off her glasses and rubbed the bridge of her nose as she headed to the front door, stiff and bleary from the long work session. She'd forgotten to set her timer for the necessary get up and stretch breaks.

Matt stood grinning in her doorway, so handsome, and soaked to the skin. "Got caught in the rain."

"Would you like a towel?"

"No, thanks. Come on, I want you to do something with me. You don't need your keys. We're just going to the corner." He caught her hand and drew her to the door.

Oh, why not? She needed a break from staring at the monitor for hours anyhow. Curious, she let him pull her along into the rain-washed yard. The sand and the pebbled driveways were flattened and dimpled from the downpour, and trees, bushes, and houses dripped and sparkled.

He led her around the corner. Water flooded the road, lapping over the curb.

"Kick off your shoes. We're going wading."

"You're crazy."

"I'm having a total flashback to boyhood. Come on, wade with me. We have to do this."

Laughing as he tugged on her, she kicked off her sandals and waded into the bathwater-warm flooded street. This had to be completely unsanitary.

Matt kept her hand in his, wading closer to the drowned storm drain. "The puddle feels just like it did when we were kids. I think it's even deeper this time than I remember. I kind of expected it to feel shallower."

The water swished around her calves. "How about that? I would have guessed the same. I wonder if it's because the town stripped and repaved the street a few years ago."

Passersby were shooting them odd looks and then joining in the laughter, as if struck by the urge to do the same crazy thing. Yes, Matt and she were two adults acting like silly kids splashing around in the huge puddle and being silly felt incredibly good and freeing.

Katie grinned broadly. "Mom would be so incredibly grossed out by us doing this."

Matt swept a foot through the water, kicking up small wakes. "I bet. I keep expecting to hear her yell at us to get out of the street. I just couldn't pass this up. Weird how I was remembering this the other day and today it rains hard enough to make it happen."

He spun and kissed her firm and fast. "I wish the old merry-go-round was still there."

"We could really make it fly now."

"Absolutely."

A car honked at them, rounding the corner too fast and too close.

"Guess we better get out of the street."

"Safer, and probably the major reason Mom always yelled at us, beside the swarming hordes of germs."

"True. Getting flattened would put a definite kink in our day." He wrapped his arm around her waist, and they headed for the curb.

Matt's arm around her fit perfectly, as if he belonged there. Only, allowing herself to get used to that feeling would be risky. He was leaving.

"You know what we need to do now?"

"What?" She slipped her feet into her sandals and wrinkled her nose at the irritating sand grains sticking between her wet toes.

"We need to get some ice cream."

"I really need to get back to work." However, steamy memories of his teasing licks over her fingers and his searing gaze sent her insides clenching with need and her tone filled with surrender.

"Walk with me for ice cream, and then I'll let you get back to work. Promise."

"Oh, okay. I could use the walk. I've been sitting all day glued to my computer." Anyhow, she'd forgotten to eat lunch.

"Great."

Matt kept his arm around her as they walked to Jimmies and Sprinkles, stirring up strange emotions, as if she'd found something she'd never known she'd lost, as if they'd always done this, when they hadn't taken a walk together after a rainstorm in twenty long years. And when they had, they certainly hadn't walked embraced like lovers.

The chill air conditioning of the ice cream shop was a welcome relief from the heat, and studying the long list of flavors allowed Katie some escape from her thoughts.

Matt scanned the board once more. "So, what flavor today? We went traditional yesterday."

"I usually get strawberry and vanilla."

"I'll get something crazy if you will."

"Oh, okay, but I have no idea." The shop offered too many flavors and possible combinations. "How about an amaretto and espresso twist?"

"Sounds tasty. Then I'll go for the black cherry and cheesecake."

This time she played it safe, skipped the sugar cone, and ordered her ice cream in a cup with a spoon. No opening the door to finger licking opportunities today, however fascinating.

She sat at one of the small iron tables by the front window and Matt slipped into the opposite seat.

"Ready for the taste test?" He'd also ordered his in a cup and waited, spoon poised.

She scooped up a spoonful and let the sweet, rich mouthful melt over her tongue. "Yum, like dessert at an Italian restaurant."

"We should do that tonight. I haven't been to a good Italian place in a while. Any places you recommend?"

"Ah, there's one in Point Pleasant Beach. Emilia's"

"It's a date then. We'll go there."

The date word sent her mind stuttering as she watched him take a bite of his ice cream. Sensations of his kisses flowed through her.

Snap out of it.

Blushing, she focused on his face. He was watching her with that amused, knowing look in his eyes again. He dug back into his ice cream, but offered her the spoonful.

Knowing better, but unwilling to resist the impulse, she leaned forward and closed her mouth over the creamy bite, meeting Matt's gaze. His eyes darkened and he swallowed hard. She slipped the mouthful free, savoring the rich black cherry, cream cheese, and vanilla.

Two could play at this teasing game. She scooped a spoonful of her ice cream, still locking eyes with Matt, and offered up the bite. As he drew off the mouthful, the sharp coil of desire in her belly filled her with pleasure and anxiety.

This was simply flirting, wasn't it? Flirting was supposedly safe, but this felt more like speeding down the Parkway, knowing you'd lost your brakes.

~*~

Matt caught his breath, never having intended this simple ice cream treat to turn so heated between them, but this is what he was wanting to see, Katie desiring him as much as he desired her.

He cleared his throat. "So, tell me more about this restaurant, Emilia's. Is it near the boardwalk? Do we need reservations?"

"Well, it's in town. You need reservations on the weekend, but midweek we should be okay. The food's very fresh, with a good selection of lighter entrees and original seafood dishes on top of the traditional items like lasagna and veal parmigiana. They're BYOB, so if you'd like wine with dinner, we'll need to bring a bottle along. Oh, and their breadbasket! They have the best bread."

"I can't wait to check them out. We'll stop in at the liquor store on our way home and pick out something you'd like. Do they serve dessert?"

A dreamy expression filled her face, and she groaned happily. "Emilia's makes an amazing tiramisu and the best espresso. They also have this yummy zabaglione with fresh strawberries. Completely worth every last outrageous calorie"

Would Katie have that same savoring look in bed? Because he wanted her under him, wanted to be deep within her, wanted to give her everything he could to make her look at him the same way as when she was remembering those desserts.

Watching her mouth close on her spoon, over and over, was pleasant torture, but walking out of the shop without embarrassment once they finished their ice cream might be tricky. He hoped his untucked shirt was up to the task.

Katie decided she was in the mood for red wine, and they found a good bottle of Chianti at the liquor store. She let him hold her hand all the way home.

Letting her go at her porch steps was difficult, but he behaved. "How much more time do you need to work? What time would you like to leave for the restaurant?"

Confusion flitted over her face. She sucked in a

deep breath, coming back from wherever her thoughts had dragged her. "I could use a couple hours. Could we make it six?"

Had she been thinking of her husband?

Stop. Enough of this absurd jealousy. The man is dead, and she's going out with you tonight.

"Six it is. Good luck with your project." He brushed a quick kiss to her mouth and left her on the porch.

Matt was washed, shaved, dressed, and knocking at Katie's door at six.

Katie opened the door and stole his breath away. She wore one of her summery dresses, this one sky blue and clinging to every curve, the deep scoop of the neckline dipping to reveal a tempting glimpse of cleavage, and the knee-skimming skirt drawing his eye down long legs to a pair of fancy sandals decorated with silver seashells. She'd done her hair up in a casual knot that let soft curls dangle and tempt his fingers. More silver seashells glinted at her earlobes and rosy lipstick accentuated her mouth.

Be careful what you ask for . . .

He swallowed, suddenly dry-mouthed and extremely turned on. "You look incredible."

Katie smiled. "Thanks."

Desperately shoving away the impulse to suggest skipping supper, he jammed his hands in his pockets and turned toward the car. "I, ah, checked the weather. Looks like we're done with rain for today."

"We should have a lovely evening then."

"Did you make progress on your project?"

"Pretty good. I'm happy with how it's coming

along. Just hope my client is as pleased."

He opened the car door for her. "I'm sure they will be."

He'd checked out her website and cruised through her portfolio of work. If he ever needed to have a website designed or other graphics work, she'd be the one he'd call.

Emilia's was located in the small, but busy center of Point Pleasant Beach, and they had to park three blocks away, but that gave him an excuse to catch Katie's hand in his as they walked the tree-lined street.

The food was as delicious as Katie had promised, the Chianti perfectly complemented their entrees, and they shared bites of the decadent tiramisu and zabaglione. However, it was Katie who made his evening perfect: her sparkling eyes, her laughter, the light and easy flirting as their shared simple conversation and nonsense. He'd never been more certain about wanting a woman in his life. Katie was the one for him.

Before heading back to the car, they strolled around town holding hands, looking in all the shop windows. They stopped at the candy shop to watch saltwater taffy being hand-pulled. As a kid, he'd always begged for the taffy, but he passed tonight, despite the pleasant lure of nostalgia. Instead, he bought them each a dark chocolate truffle for a treat, brandied black cherry for himself and apricot for Katie.

"Should we head to the car or do you want to keep walking?" He teased his lips over her mouth, enjoying how she softened and joined whole-heartedly into their kiss. The busy street faded away.

"Kate? Oh, it is you!"

At the brisk, friendly call, Katie flinched away from Matt, panic filling her eyes before she smoothed her expression and turned to face the woman.

A smiling couple strode up, the redheaded woman's sharp blue gaze scouting over them both before she wrapped Katie in a hug with a kiss to the cheek. "What fun running into you here tonight!"

"Hey, Nadine. What a surprise." Katie returned the woman's hug and gave the blond man a hearty embrace. "Hi, Tony. Good to see you."

Nadine locked intent eyes on Matt. "And who's this?"

Katie laughed tensely and curled her hands behind her.

"Ah, Nadine, this is an old friend of mine, Matt Powell, from Seattle. Matt, this is my sister-in-law Nadine Wescott, ah, Jeb's sister, and her husband Tony."

Matt stepped in and shook hands with the couple. "Nice to meet you."

"So, Matt, have you known our Kate long?" Nadine continued eying him as if he were an alien specimen up for possible dissection.

He caught Katie's hand and laced his fingers into hers, concerned by her tension. "Since we were eight. My grandparents used to own the house next to hers. We lost touch when we were teens. I got bit by the nostalgia bug and decided to rent the old place. Finding Katie again was a complete and happy surprise."

Suspicion eased, but didn't completely

disappear from Nadine's eyes. She'd most definitely witnessed their kiss. "I bet. What are you two up to tonight?"

Katie answered. "We had a lovely dinner at Emilia's and were just heading back to Lavallette."

"Oh, how funny! We were out to dinner with Mikki and Ray and Cami and Brent, and we almost ate there tonight, but Mikki was craving Chinese."

"How's Mikki doing? I haven't talked to Cami in a couple weeks."

"She's doing great, but she's so huge already. I can't believe she's having twins. She and Ray are having no luck with the new house hunt." Nadine shook her head with a grimace. "Brent was tedious as always, glued to his phone. I have no idea what Cami sees in him—Hey, I have an idea! We were heading home to relieve the babysitter, but we don't have to rush off. Let's have some coffee together first."

Katie's hand tightened, but she turned to him. "Sure, if Matt is up for it."

He didn't read a plea in her face for him to say no, and he was curious about her seemingly friendly in-laws. "Coffee sounds good."

The coffee and conversation proved more enjoyable than he feared from Katie's tension, and they ended up spending over an hour with Nadine and Tony. Nadine was edgy and a touch abrasive, but seemed deeply fond of Katie, and he enjoyed talking with her about her work as a director for a children's literacy organization. Tony was as quiet and steady as he first appeared, but livened up when talking about sports, his job teaching history at the Point Pleasant High School, and their three small children. The antics of their two girls and boy spurred lively talk and Katie clearly loved being their aunt.

Nadine hugged Katie goodnight. "Call me. We need to get together for lunch soon, just you and me. It's been too long." Her happy smile thinned. "Oh, and heads up, Kate. Mom's been rumbling about getting us all together for a Sunday dinner. You'll come, right?"

Katie smiled sweetly, with only her eyes revealing the tension revving back to full force. "Of course. Just let me know when and what to bring."

On the drive back to Lavallette, Katie was quiet, and Matt puzzled over the conflicting vibes surrounding her and her sister-in-law. Well, losing a husband and a brother would punch holes into any family dynamic.

A more sobering consideration followed. If his plans for Katie and him succeeded, her folks would be affected by their decisions, as would those in-laws who would remain connected to Katie. He'd have to find his place in that disturbed dynamic, further disturbed by his taking her away from them.

Not an issue. He'd deal and make it work. Katie was worth whatever troubles rose.

He parked in his driveway and walked her to her front door.

"I had a wonderful time tonight. Thank you." She paused at the door, keys clenched in her hand. "Well, have a good night."

"I had a great time, too." He slipped his arm around her and drew her into a kiss.

This time she joined in without hesitation, and their kiss sizzled, sweet and slow. This time he let himself fill his need to touch her, grazing his hands greedily over her curves, nestling her body close into his, and relishing her eager rise and press into his touch.

He threw all his need into the brain-spinning kiss, but still, he needed more. Cupping her breast, he savored the full heaviness, the nipple tight and prominent under his thumb. He groaned, frustrated at the clothes keeping them from the skin-to-skin contact he craved.

"Oh, Katie, how I need you." His voice cracked in a ragged growl. He tasted kisses over her soft throat. "Invite me in. Please."

She fisted her hands against his chest, catching her breath with a whimper.

His heart sank. He'd spoken too soon and broken the mood.

"Matt, I . . ." She rested her cheek against his shoulder and shook her head. "It's been a wonderful day, but I'm sorry. I need to say goodnight. I—I'm not ready for this. I'm too confused. I need to think." She pushed at his embrace.

Frustration burned, but he let her slip from his arms.

Katie backed against the door, staring up at him, eyes huge and hurting.

He'd do anything to make that look go away. He cupped her cheek, hating her stressed shiver. "Sleep well. I had a great night." He brushed his lips over her mouth, plucked the keys from her hand, opened the door, and stepped away. "I'll see you tomorrow."

Leaving Katie with that pain in her eyes was tough, but he turned away as she needed him to and walked down the steps, past the mailbox bearing her dead love's name, and towards the dark, empty house next door.

He really should remember to leave a light on.

Chapter Six

*K*ATIE FLOPPED ON HER BED WITH A FRUSTRATED groan and kicked off her sandals.

Maybe a cup of herbal tea and a shower would help her relax.

Matt would have helped you relax.

Memories of his massaging her neck and shoulders raised a heated flush. Oh, she could use hands right now. If she hadn't been so foolishly scared, she'd have that comfort and pleasure and so much more. Matt could drive the fear and loss and pain away, if she were willing to risk believing his plea to stay meant more than a passing affair together.

Oh, come on. Remember you keep saying you aren't ready for this whatever is happening between you two? Remember where falling too fast for the influence of sweet words and heady kisses led you last time?

Right, she'd made the intelligent decision in turning Matt down tonight.

But, she wanted him so much.

Oh . . . and running into Nadine and Tony. Oh, boy, oh, boy. She pressed a palm to her forehead. Had Nadine seen that little kiss? Well, more than little kiss. Worse, she'd been caught without her rings. Would Nadine tell her mother Marie that Kate had been out on a date, wasn't wearing Jeb's rings, and had kissed a man in public?

She was so weary of all the subterfuge. She cared about Jeb's family and hated to hurt their feelings—even after nearly four years they all were still grieving—but she wanted freedom from this fictional bubble of denial and living a lie with them because they refused to see, didn't want to know that Jeb was anything but their lost hero, their good boy.

Maybe Matt was what she needed to break free. Maybe she could use him—Well, not *use* Matt, but allow this romantic shift in their friendship to give her the excuse to fully move on with her life, and more, spur a change to this draining emotional trap with the MacBains into something more . . . healthy.

Matt is leaving. You're going to hurt all over again.

No, stop being pessimistic. Focus on this night. Matt wanted her, as a man wants a woman. That was so clear, and if she'd been denying the clues before, well, his asking tonight was proof.

But did Matt want more than just her body? She was afraid to risk giving her crushed and cracked heart away again. They'd known each other completely once, but life had changed them. She'd loved Matt, hadn't ever stopped, but that old love was as a little girl for a little boy. This thing happening now, this was huge and different.

Well, you didn't know Jeb so completely as you believed either.

Even more reason she was right to worry.

How on earth had Jeb been so casual and careless with his affairs? How could he be so loving to her, yet love the others?

Despite years of chewing over this question, she still failed to see where they'd had a problem. They'd been great in bed together. Absolutely no issues there in the lovemaking area. They'd had fun together. They got along so well. They never fought, barely disagreed. Why had Jeb needed those other women?

She laughed, sick and despairing. How had Jeb had the time?

What if she just gave in and accepted whatever Matt offered, for however long their reunion lasted, whether it was a week or a few fun months or longer?

What if she just released the grief, guilt, and anger, simply trusted her feelings for Matt, both the old and the new, took the leap, and moved on?

She would sleep on possibilities and examine how she felt in the daylight when she wasn't aching for kisses in the dark.

If she could sleep.

Sleep came hard, but she managed a few straight hours before the mockingbird launched into its operatic warmup.

She dragged downstairs and made coffee. So, what would she do today? Hide from Matt or tackle the issue head on? Attempt to act like normal friends together? Sit down and discuss this attraction between them like sensible adults?

Sadly, she felt far more like an anxious child than a sensible adult.

Her phone rang, and her scattered thoughts made her pick up without first checking the caller ID.

"Good morning." Concern radiated in Matt's warm voice. "I just wanted to check and see if you were okay."

She took a deep breath. "I'm fine. It's, well, there's a lot to take in."

"I can't apologize for wanting you, but I am sorry if I pushed too hard. Do you have to work today?"

Avoiding Matt solves nothing. Stand up. Face it. Move on.

"I really should put some time in this morning."

She sucked in another breath against the anxious and desirous butterflies currently warring in her belly. She'd be a liar if she claimed she hadn't been madly tempted by his kiss last night.

Take that step. Do it.

"But I should be done by noon, if you'd like to get together then."

"I would like. Very much. Have anything you'd like to do on this sunny Wednesday?"

"I'm game, for whatever you think of." She winced as she took two filets from the freezer in case they decided on dinner at home. Oh, boy, that offer could be taken many ways.

He chuckled. "Okay, I'll bring you lunch, and we'll see what comes next."

Despite her distraction, she managed to buckle

down and be productive. Her client loved the header, and she had several new inquiries from referrals. New clients always made her happy.

The morning flew, and before she knew it, Matt's "Hello, lunch is here!" rang out from her kitchen.

"Be right there."

He was already setting out the food when she joined him in the kitchen: fried clams, shrimp, and calamari, a big container of coleslaw, and French fries. He'd even picked up the small cups of tartar sauce, marinara sauce, and hot sauce for dipping.

"Oh, wow, it smells delicious."

"I drove down to Seaside and stopped in at Salty's Shack. Hopefully, everything's still crunchy. I waited until the last minute to pick up the order and get back here."

"My diet wants to hit you, and my taste buds want to hug you. Salty's food is so terrible and so delicious."

He grinned. "I'll take the hug."

Her heart swelled with happy, confused desire, and she wrapped him in a hug. Having Matt in her arms felt so wonderful and so right.

Keeping her close, he leaned over, snagged a fried shrimp, and teased the treat in front of her lips. "You know you want this."

She bit down on the crunchy, fattening morsel and groaned. "Oh, so good. I haven't had this in absolute ages."

"I brought beer too. I behaved, though, and skipped the funnel cakes."

He popped the tops on the bottles, passed her one, and raised his. "Here's to a great Wednesday."

She tapped her bottle to his. "Cheers." She took a long, fizzy sip of the pleasant lager. "So, did you decide what you want to do with the rest of the day?"

"Well, after this lunch, we probably won't want to do much but lay around." He popped a fry into his mouth. "Oh, that's good." He groaned, and fed her a fry before freeing her to sit at the table.

He scooped coleslaw onto their plates. "Since the weather forecast promises a perfect afternoon, we can go laze around at the beach, look for sea glass, and swim a little."

"Lazy sounds perfect."

By the time they finished, their stomachs were groaning, but content. Matt had his beach gear ready, and he waited on the porch while Katie changed into her swimsuit and packed her bag.

This time up at the beach, when she asked him to put sunscreen on her back, she allowed herself to enjoy every second of his rubbing the lotion over her body. This time he let her do the same for him, and she eagerly seized the pleasurable opportunity to touch and explore the strong stretch of his muscular shoulders and back. This time when they napped side by side in the sun, he closed his hand around hers.

After their short nap and the drowsy effects of the heavy lunch had worn off, they went swimming, flirting together in the buoyant, warm water. She let him steal light, salty kisses as she stole touches and hugs, bodies brushing together and pulling away under the rocking tide.

Afterwards, they lounged in the sun until they felt like walking the waterline to search for sea glass and shells. They found one worn piece of blue glass and a perfect white scallop shell.

The sun was throwing long shadows from rooftops when they gathered towels and bags and began their sandy walk back to the house hand in hand.

~*~

As they approached Katie's house, her grip tensed on Matt's hand, and the soft relaxation in her face shifted to unsettled thought. Matt sighed, resigned to the fact Jeb had intruded between them again.

After separate showers, he joined her in the kitchen where they started preparing supper while sharing snacks and had a drink.

Matt knew what he wanted. Katie.

Yes, this desire for her complicated everything. Yes, this desire was crazy, unexpected, and disturbing—and inspiring and exciting, and growing ever more profound and intense. This desire definitely complicated the career decision he had to make. He should really want this to be a passing thing between them, but their deepening connection felt far from temporary.

Avoiding the decision was avoiding progress. On one hand, having three firms panting after him to join them was very nice for the ego. On the other hand, having choices was a real pain because any decision on a firm in turn utterly complicated the decisions he needed to make about Katie.

His stomach gave a grinding, acid twist. Shit, how he dreaded jumping back into the work grind.

Enough. He shoved that problematic admission to the rear of his mind. Career decisions were for next week. Today was all about Katie and he being together now.

So then, it's simple here. You want her. You two will make love or not make love, but either way, be prepared to accept the consequences of your action or non-action.

Choices. So, concede politely to Katie's understandably conflicted feelings, back off, and suffer this ill-timed attraction silently, or act on the undeniable desire they shared, make his own feelings clear and deal with the repercussions as they arose?

He leaned back in his chair, enjoying the view of Katie working in the kitchen. She was humming an unfamiliar, happy tune as she chopped veggies for the salad. Her glasses kept slipping down her nose. Yes, this thing with Katie had complicated his life, but so much gave him happiness. He even loved her little impatient scrunch of her nose and finger push at the bridge of her glasses.

She peeked through the oven window to check her au gratin potatoes and straightened with a smile. "I think we can start the steaks."

"Good. The grill should be nice and hot now."

He picked up the plate of marinated steaks and headed outside.

Complications aside, he hadn't been this happy and content in forever. All thanks to Katie.

Matt kept himself in check through supper, enjoying the peaceful meal with her and even the cleaning up afterwards. He wanted this peace and companionship. He wanted this simple time together as much as he wanted her in his bed. He wanted both. He wanted meals with her, to wash dishes with her, and just sit on the porch with her.

He wanted to see her in evening light and see her smile first thing in the morning.

You want to kiss her. So kiss her.

He laid a hand on her shoulder, turning her from the dried dish she had set on the counter. The sunset light pouring through the kitchen window cast a warm glow over her smiling face and added delicate glints of fire to her hair. Without a word, he slipped off her glasses and set them aside. Her eyes widened. He grazed one hand over her cheek as he caught his other hand around her waist and lowered his lips to hers.

A soft gasp escaped her, and she stiffened for a long worrisome moment, but then settled into his kiss and embrace.

Good. He took his time, brushing his mouth to hers, giving soft presses and nibbles, drawing her close, and settling her in his arms. He leaned back against the counter, cradling her between his legs, leaving the way clear for her to feel she had an escape, but putting his all into the kiss to convince her to stay.

She dropped the towel, and as her hands slipped up to grip his shoulders, she sighed and yielded to the kiss.

Even if there was no doubt in his mind or body that he wanted in her bed, this was good. He wanted to do whatever she wanted, even if all they did was kiss. He'd make tonight as perfect as he could for *her*. He wanted to help her find a way to stow her pain and yearnings for her dead husband in long-term storage. He wanted to ensure she wasn't thinking about the past, loss, change, or regret. He wanted to see her laugh and smile because he was giving her everything she wanted in her present. He wanted to wipe away her grief and fill her with pleasure.

Realizing how his goals had shifted from pursuing his frustrated desires to worrying over her needs rocked him—and, damn, how that amazing shift made him more determined to give her his all.

This was *his* Katie, the Katie who'd meant more to him than anyone when he was a kid. The Katie who'd understood him like no one else had. The Katie who'd made him feel he fit into the world. She had been his special, singular friend, and that childhood adoration had just detonated beyond simple physical desire into something powerful, heavy, and immense.

Love?

Could he love Katie, not just desire her? He'd been sadly less than adept at loving so far in his life. He felt safe in saying he loved his sister and niece deeply, but that sentiment for them was still a neat and tidy emotion. The wild emotions currently careening around in his chest and brain felt too complex for such a simple word as love.

Trailing kisses down Katie's throat, he savored her soft skin, her pulse beating fast under his lips, her sigh, and clenching fingers tugging him closer. Bursting with the need to tell her how he felt, how incredible he found her, he feared breaking the magic of the moment with mere words. He'd show her. That he could do.

Loving the perfect fit of her body pliant against his, her tiny sighs and gasps, he kissed his way past her collarbone and to the swells of her breasts above the V of her knit dress.

Damn, how he loved her summer dresses and how the low necklines skimmed the lacy edges of her colorful bras. He loved how his former tomboy Katie was now this feminine, flowery, lingerie-loving woman.

He kissed her gorgeous cleavage, raising one hand to cup her breast and stroke his thumb over her tightly budded nipple. She whimpered and wriggled against him, arching to press into his hand.

Slipping his fingers beneath the strap of her dress, he gently nudged the dress and bra straps to slide from her shoulder and slowly bare one breast, but she gave no effort to halt his exploration. He cupped his hand around the warm, soft handful of her breast, the creamy curves and rosy nipple so damned beautiful. A shiver ran through her. A glance at her face found her eyes closed, mouth softly parted, and expression yearning.

A pang struck him. She might be pretending her dead husband was the one touching her.

Shit. Didn't matter. *He* was the one who'd put that look on her face. He would give her everything he had in him to give. If she needed to pretend he was Jeb for now, so be it. He couldn't demand she forget her lost love, but he planned to make damned sure she knew he wasn't Jeb, and that the man making love to her was living, breathing flesh and blood. He had no intentions of being just a fond memory anymore and if he needed to share her with a ghost, he'd find a way to deal.

He shifted and replaced his stroking thumb with his mouth, drawing her in and rolling her against his tongue.

She jolted, softly crying out, "Matt!" Clinging

tighter, she rode against him, her hands clasping his head.

That simple cry, that she knew exactly who was making love to her charged him. His heart filled to bursting.

"Aw, Katie, my Katie."

~*~

My Katie.

Yes, all Katie could think clearly was *yes, yes, yours.*

Yes, she wanted Matt's kisses. If she had any sense, she'd gently push Matt away and end this looming mistake. However, thinking she should was all she could manage.

Oh, yes, how she wanted more.

Yes, she wanted to see passion in a man's eyes again and be swept off her feet! She was so tired of being alone and untouched and unkissed.

He tugged her closer. No mistaking his intent now. Or hers, as she eagerly rose and rode against his rigid arousal. At his encouraging groan, her pulse leapt. She laced her fingers into his hair, pulling into the incredible luscious suckling of his hot mouth.

So what if this was about to be the second stupidest thing she'd done in her life—Oh, no, untrue, this had to be most foolish, because, unlike falling in love with Jeb, this time she knew better.

"You're so damned beautiful."

Another groan rumbled through him, and he pushed her dress down, freeing both breasts, and scorched her with a consuming, eye-crossing suckling of her breast, now teasing her wet nipple between his fingers as he bit and sucked at her other breast.

That deep yearning ache tightened, heat filled her, and her heart pounded.

She dropped her hands to his shoulders, skimming the strong shapes of bone and muscle, caressing down the solid planes of his back to the tail of his shirt and up beneath the hem to slide her hands over the delicious heat of his smooth skin.

In one fast move, he broke away, stripped the polo shirt over his head, and reclaimed her mouth, hands on her rear, crushing her closer. They'd shifted around, locked together in the heady kiss and now her back was against the cool fridge door. She wriggled her arms free, letting her dress and bra fall to her hips.

Then he cupped her breast again, flicking a thumb against her nipple, and she cried out under the pure jolt of bliss. He chuckled and stroked her again.

"Oh, yes. Oh, Matt."

Sparkling filled her eyes. Dazed with pleasure, she sluggishly realized her sun catcher was swaying in a breeze, and she was naked from the waist up in full view of the large kitchen window.

"Window! Matt, the window."

"What? Oh, right." After a groaning laugh, he scooped her into his arms and carted her out of the kitchen. "Where to?"

Oh, she was really committing to this, wasn't she?

Katie swallowed hard. Last chance to stay no, but she still wanted him with frightening intensity. Time to take the leap and move on. "Yes. Upstairs. My room."

Thank goodness she'd tidied her room this morning. Wait, he only knew her former little room in the back.

"Um, it's in the front room now."

Admittedly still unsettled as he carried her up the stairs, but determined to trust all her feelings for Matt, she focused on cruising kisses over his neck. She sucked on a sensitive place beneath his jaw, loving how he groaned and tightened his hands on her.

"Ah, feels so good, Katie."

He lowered her to the bed, taking her mouth again in a searing kiss and laying her back, before he broke away and stood. With slow deliberation, he slipped her fallen dress off and unclasped her bra, draping both neatly around the bedpost.

Feeling a wild mix of excited and terribly bare, Katie lay arms flung out and calves dangling off the edge of the bed, her breasts rising and falling with her breathless gasps. Only her lace panties remained, a fragile shield against his intense perusal.

Tension filled Matt's face and his broad shoulders, and his erection strained against his shorts. His serious brows lowered. His voice rolled out, dark and ragged.

"I'm half out of my mind with wanting you, Katie, but you have to tell me you want *me*. I need to know you're sure of this. That you want *me* to be here with you."

Tenderness flared, wanting to ease his worries. "I want to be here with you, Matt. I want you."

"Thank you." He released a rush of breath, and his grave expression warmed.

Keeping his eyes locked on her, he removed a condom from his wallet and set both aside on her night table. He unfastened his shorts, shoving them down and stepped free.

Still lying flung open to his view, Katie looked her fill in turn, admiring every inch of him and marveling how a thin boy had filled out into such a passionate, handsome man. The brushing of brown hair over his chest tapered into an arrow drawing her gaze down his flat abdomen to the darker lower curls and that once unknown part of him, now no more a concealed need, but hard and erect.

One long step brought him to the bed, his legs brushing against hers. He caught the band of her panties and drew them off, setting them aside with her dress and bra.

She was open, bare, naked, and he gazed and gazed, face filled with a burning, awe-tinged desire.

"Oh, Katie, you are so beautiful."

"Kiss me." She held out her hand to him.

He stepped back between her knees and took her hand. He leaned over her, braced on his hands, and rained her with kisses as if some restraint had been freed within him, kissing and licking at her mouth, her breasts, and down her ticklish belly, laughing at her giggles and teasing her more.

Then, he caught her legs, spreading them as he dropped to his knees and brought his mouth down on her center, his tongue and lips testing and driving her wild with the delicious sensual torment.

Flushing and pleading for him to stop and to keep going. It had been too long, and this was so, so good. Shuddering, she gave herself over to the wrenching waves of pleasure.

When she drifted happily back to herself, he was kissing her mouth, telling her all sorts of ardent, loving nonsense, his deep voice all sweet and rough.

Then, he lifted away and covered himself. How his hands shook shot delight through her. *She'd* made him feel that way.

He caught her up, tumbling them over in bed, and guiding her down over him, filling her steady and slow and deep, thick and long, stretching her, his hands tightening on her hips, his eyes locked on hers. Rocking and rising, withdrawing and filling. Finding their rhythm together was easy, the slow friction so perfect. This, this, yes.

Then slow snapped. Need ruled. They moved faster and deeper, rough and desperate together. He hauled her forward, latching his mouth on her breast, suckling hard. He filled her full and perfect.

Sensation pierced her, delight coiling hot and sharp. Grinding down on him as he drove up into her, her fingers biting his shoulders, she strained for the shimmering edge. Her thighs shaking, her breath harsh, she cried for more.

So close, so close—

He surged harder, thrust deeper, his eyes bright, his jaw locked in a satisfied grin.

"Matt!" And with that, she lost control, the blessed orgasm cascaded over her, and she distantly noted her very loud pleasured cry.

"Katie, love, yes!" He growled and dragged her close and fierce, driving on, his face and body taut under the strain of his own release.

Katie collapsed against Matt, gasping against his neck, totally shattered in the most beautiful way.

His chest heaved and his heart pounded a rapid

beat in time with hers, sweat gluing them together as he wrapped her tightly in his arms. He gulped air, his body relaxing under her into exhausted peace, but not his possessive grip.

Amazed, astounded, overjoyed—if only she could catch her breath and find the words to thank him.

Chapter Seven

*M*ATT TIGHTENED HIS ARMS AROUND KATIE AND stroked a hand along her spine. He breathed deep, slowing his ragged pants. If only he could hang onto this state of satisfied exhaustion, this intense happiness. He replayed the beauty of her riding him, the passion on her face, the connection between them that was far more than just their bodies.

"That was incredible, thank you, thank you," she murmured in his ear.

Incredible was far from close. He'd known they'd be good together, but this additional unexpected explosion of emotion . . . the pleasure had rocketed beyond mere physical release.

"You're welcome. Very much my pleasure."

Her gentle laughter sent a warm, joyous surge through him. Rolling them to their side, he delayed separating from her for a moment longer as he looked into her smiling eyes, full of the unexpected rush of being home in *her*. Speechless with the thought, he channeled all these confused happy feelings into a kiss.

Eventually, pulling away to clean up was necessary. "Be right back."

She smiled, eyes dreamy, eyelids drifting closed, her face rosy and soft.

Loving Katie. Love . . . If this stunning fresh feeling was love, he'd never be able to let her go.

His Katie. Face it, letting go was no longer an option.

He headed downstairs and grabbed two glasses and the bottle of Riesling from the fridge.

Yes, decisions lay ahead, but not tonight. Tonight would be all about loving Katie. He'd save rational thought for another day.

Back upstairs, he found Katie curled into the pillows, charmingly rumpled and relaxed, eyes closed, and her lips softly set in a drowsy curve.

As he glanced around her tidy bedroom decorated in a light and cheerful shore theme, a disquieting prickle rose along his spine at the odd absence of any photos of Jeb.

Admittedly, he could happily live without a photo of the guy staring at them as he made love to Katie, but the complete lack of even the smallest snapshot anywhere in her house was wrong. This kind of trouble would drive him to digging even deeper into a case to discover who was hiding what and why.

Enough. Do the photos matter right here and now?

No. That was definitely another question best left for daylight.

As he settled onto the bed and poured the wine, Katie opened her eyes and smiled.

"Oh, wine, how lovely." She wriggled up to sit against the piled pillows and accepted a glass.

"Not as lovely as you." He sipped his wine, drinking in the sight of her beautiful, naked body, her kiss-bruised mouth, and the happiness shining in her eyes.

She laughed, shaking a splash of her wine over the rim. He leaned over and licked the sweet spill from her skin, following the rolling droplet to her nipple, savoring the honeyed apricot flavor of the wine and richer taste of Katie.

Struck by impulse, he grinned and dribbled another small spill between her breasts.

"Matt!" She squealed and laughed.

He chuckled, chasing the racing rivulet to her navel with his tongue.

Her giggles and laughter filled him with ever-richer happiness as he lapped up each new spill with licks and kisses. Again and again, he teased and tasted every inch of Katie, until the wine was gone, her eyes were deep, and her giggles were now sweet moans and pleas.

She tugged him to her impatiently. "I need you. Now!"

And he needed her. He filled her, drunk on the joy of making love to Katie once more.

This time they cuddled afterwards and fell asleep in each other's arms. Matt slept solidly and peacefully until the mockingbird's crack-of-dawn choir practice woke him to the pure pleasure of Katie naked against his back, her arm wrapped around his waist. Her soft waking kiss to his shoulder led to more loving in the cool of morning, sweet, peaceful, and perfect.

After a nap, they made their way into the shower and then downstairs for breakfast.

Katie relaxed in her chair sipping at her coffee. "What are your plans for the day? I need to put a few hours of work in, but if all goes smoothly we could do something together this afternoon, if you like?"

"No plans but laziness. Maybe read. Maybe go up to the beach."

"Sounds good. I'll let you think of what you'd like to do this afternoon. I'll give you a ring when I'm finishing up, and then you can tell me what you've planned."

One last, long kiss, and he left her to her work. While he'd rather lounge in bed with Katie, he was looking forward to kicking back on the sofa and reading. Reading for pleasure was an activity he'd had no time for far too long. Also, it was Thursday already. His fleeting time-out was almost half over. Today might also be a good time to start weighing his choices, adding in the fact of Katie, and at least eliminate one firm from his options. A walk to the drugstore was also in order.

So read, take a walk, and then crack down on some planning.

He scooped up the paperback, set his phone on the coffee table on the off-chance Katie finished working early, and stretched out on the sofa, sighing into the pleasant weariness. Despite the intriguing suspense plot, he was out like a light after two chapters and slept until just after noon.

So much for reading. He pried himself from the

couch and headed off on his walk to the drugstore, the seafood shop, and the ice cream shop for the few things he needed, along with stop at the liquor store for a nice bottle of pinot grigio to replace the wine they'd finished.

Playing with the wine and Katie last night had been surprising fun. He'd never done something so let loose and gone with the moment in his adult life. He liked the feeling.

More, he liked his entire sense of wellbeing over these past days. His neck had been pain-free, and he hadn't needed to pop even one antacid in over a week. Last month, eating a fried lunch like the one they'd shared yesterday would have killed his digestive system. He felt high and revved, everything was working out, and with Katie in his life again, the future looked even brighter than he hoped.

When he'd first walked out of McCollister, Janowitz, and DiTommaso, he'd felt as if he'd been released from chains. He'd stood firm on his ideals and ethics, turned his back on McCollister's snide taunts of a being a naïve dreamer, and walked out, free from the firm's cases and practices that had irked his standards, freed from the petty jealousies and backbiting, free of *everything*. That decision had been one of the top moments in his life.

Finding Katie made that decision perfect and right.

A new rung upward in his career and love in his life. Life couldn't be better.

His cell phone rang with Katie on the line.

Her voice was sweetly breathy and shy. "Hi, Matt, I'm done for the day. Come on over whenever you're ready."

"Great. I'll be there in a couple minutes." He knew exactly what he wanted to do with Katie, and every plan involved staying home.

He launched off the couch, grabbed the bottle of wine and the sack of groceries, and headed over to Katie with a bounce in his step and bubbling with happy expectation.

She met him at the door with a kiss and wrapped him in her arms.

Still kissing, he backed her into the kitchen, meaning to drop the bags on the table, but they bumped into the fridge. They burst into laughter, but stayed in the kiss—until the grocery bags slid from his hand, hitting the floor with a thud.

"Crap! The wine!"

They broke apart and Katie opened the bag. "The bottle's fine."

Matt emptied the groceries onto the table. "I picked up stuff for dinner. I thought I'd cook for you tonight." He grinned and set the package of shrimp in the fridge and pint of ice cream into the freezer.

Katie arched a brow and raised the small box from the drugstore, a smile twitching at her mouth. "Ah, is this also for dinner?"

He grinned. "That's dessert. Or the appetizer. Or both."

Her eyes twinkled, and she broke into laughter and pressed a kiss to his mouth. "We'll see."

~*~

Oh, yes, loving Matt was a perfect appetizer, dessert, and everything in between. This had to be why poets claimed you could live on love.

Katie leaned over Matt, loving the pleasure

gripping his face, his eyes shut tight in his sensual focus, loving how he was so completely into the moment. Joy and streaking heat coiled within her as she rose and tightened downward, fighting to draw out this loving as long as possible. If only she could hold onto this precious new happiness forever.

More kisses in the kitchen had exploded into crazy need and lovemaking, delaying supper, but this time they'd managed to close the blinds, thank goodness. After supper, an intent to watch the baseball game and eat ice cream on the living room sofa led to silliness, nakedness, sticky, icy play, and much laughter here in the soft nest of throw blankets on the floor.

She loved the fullness, the completion Matt gave her, the feeling they'd always been together—

Only, they hadn't.

Her rhythm stumbled, and the tightening heat of her coming release blipped into a pitiful fizzle and vanished.

Matt grabbed her hips, driving up, urging her on with rough, sweet words, too far into his own pleasure to realize she'd lost hers, barreling on to his release.

They hadn't always been together. That they'd known each other forever was a falsehood of fanciful thinking. The man beneath had been in her life six short days. Shame choked her. What was she doing having sex with a virtual stranger?

She shuddered and not from pleasure.

She didn't know Matt. They weren't in love. Chilled by a queasy surge and struck by the bizarre sensation she had just cheated on Jeb, she clutched Matt's shoulders. Yes, that was absurd, but this, this being with Matt, this wasn't like her at all.

"Katie, love—" He gripped her fiercely, his body straining, blindly lost in his orgasm.

At his simple, blissful, breathless pleasure, her tears surged, spilling hard and hot. She buried her face in his neck, futilely attempting to hide the tears.

His chest heaving, he struggled out of his languor and petted her. "Katie, hon, what's wrong? Why the tears? Tell me what's wrong."

"Sorry, sorry."

"Nothing to be sorry for. Just tell me what's wrong." His voice resonated with sweet concern.

"Just a silly tears ambush. I'll be okay. I don't even know why."

Liar, liar. You made your bed, girl, what's done is done. A little late for second thoughts.

He rolled them over, now leaning on his elbows, his expression all loving as he wiped his thumb at her tears. "You'd tell me if it was something I could help with, right?"

"Of course. As I said, just silly tears, probably just tired."

"Yeah, we didn't sleep much last night, and you worked most of the day." He brushed a kiss to her mouth. "Why don't we do this? I'll get you a brandy, we'll go upstairs and cuddle in bed and get some sleep. You'll feel better in the morning." He stretched and caught her shirt off the sofa.

The next morning, her crazed bout of nerves had passed. Doubts still niggled, but she was in a much more positive frame of mind after a surprisingly good night's sleep in Matt's arms. She'd woken wanting him fiercely, and he'd been there, right where she needed him.

Nerves, just all silly nerves. She'd have nerves in any new relationship. Once upon a time, she'd been nervous with Jeb. Relationships didn't magically snap together into perfect being. Awkwardness was bound to occur, doubts were bound to surface, but she had a choice on how to handle them. First and foremost, she had to stop allowing fear and grief to control her life.

Her mindset firmed as she dove into her work and the morning rolled along, and she felt nearly her normal self by lunchtime.

They were lazing together on the porch after lunch, both reading. Contentment had smothered most of her anxieties. Focusing on present happiness and future hopes was proving a soothing decision.

Matt set aside his book. "Remember all those stories we wrote?"

She laughed, buoyed on the sudden surging froth of happy memories. "They were so awful but so fun."

"I've thought about them from time to time over the years. We were such dreamers."

"I still have the notebooks."

"You're kidding. Really? You kept them? Can I see them?"

The joy in his face made her doubly glad she'd held onto the notebooks. "They're upstairs in a box labeled 'Stories' on the top closet shelf in the blue bedroom."

He jumped to his feet. "I'll get it."

"If you don't see it, just give a shout."

"Okay." Matt jogged eagerly upstairs.

She hadn't looked at the notebooks in forever. This would be fun, seeing the childish adventures they'd painstakingly written and illustrated.

The closet door squeaked, followed a moment later by a loud thud.

"Shit. Aw, shit."

She hurried to the stairs. "Matt, are you okay?"

"Yeah. Sorry, just knocked stuff off the shelf."

When she reached the room, she found Matt sitting on the bed, flipping through the pages of her wedding album.

He looked up, his eyes sorrowful. Pitying. "I know. I'm prying. I didn't see the album on top of the box, and I accidentally knocked it off the shelf. That was the bang. The corner is crumpled. I'm sorry."

A lump closed off her throat. Unable to speak, she sat beside him. She hadn't opened the album in years. She'd tucked it away long before Jeb died.

Wedding albums were such funny objects. Back in the beginning, they seemed so vital, so precious; you think you can never look at them enough. Time rolls by, new things take precedence, the album becomes an awkward dust-collector, and then just an item of fond memorabilia to store away out of sight and mind.

Matt turned back to the first page.

She clenched her hands together, unable to raise a protest and stop him. The lump in her throat ached to the cracking beat of her heart as the pages of her once upon a time flipped past.

How fragile life and happiness were. No shadow of the impending sorrow haunted that lovely day. The 'for worse' lines of their vows had been a warning glossed over and ignored, a vague possibility denied, and the 'till death do you part', while unavoidable, had been most emphatically expected only after long decades down the road of life.

As Matt viewed her tarnished moments of joy, he curled his hand around hers, warm and strong.

She focused on the differences. Matt's hands and fingers were narrower and longer than Jeb's. Smoother, too. Between work and play, Jeb had been so hard on his big hands, his thick fingers always sporting a bandage or two, and he'd always struggled with keeping his hands from being too dry and rough.

She made herself look at the photos of Jeb, ignoring the renewed shredding of her heart and searching his sturdy strong face. He took after his dad, with the same strawberry blond hair, his blue eyes sparkling with laughter, broad shoulders straining his tux jacket—so much the same in everything but responsibility.

How could a man who was as strong, respected, brave, and goodhearted as Jeb be so immature? How did someone supposedly so open with his feelings manage to hide so many secrets?

Matt reached the last page and the silhouette of Jeb and her in what had been a spontaneous, passionate kiss, an image that had once seemed a promise of perfect happiness for their future.

Matt shut the album and set it aside on the bed. "Thank you for letting me see these." He spoke almost in a whisper. He slipped his hand from hers and wrapped his arm around her shoulders. "I'm sorry."

She turned into him, resting her cheek against his chest and nodded. So was she, so very sorry.

"I wish I could fix this for you." He pressed a kiss to her hair, stroking his hand in gentle circles over her back. His sweetness only worsened the consuming ache. "I'm sorry you lost him."

Matt deserved to know the basics. Maybe telling him would keep him from needing to ask more. She'd found the barest facts satisfied most people, the sweeter fiction of happiness and sudden loss, edited clean of the bitter truth that loss had revealed.

"Jeb was responding to a motor vehicle accident. He stepped off the truck, ready to work on an extraction, and he just went down. An aneurysm. We'd never had a clue. One moment, working, the next moment, gone. When Simon and Jerry knocked at the door . . ."

Poor Simon, she'd known his errand the moment she'd seen his face. The pain and sorrow his eyes had held had smashed her heart.

"They told me he didn't suffer. I still waffle on whether being quick was for the best or not. I didn't get to say goodbye and from time to time, the unreality hits me hard."

A sick flare of the old anger scorched her—I didn't get to kill him myself for being a cheating jerk. I didn't get to ask him *why!*

She squared her shoulders. "The early days were rough, but it's been nearly four years, and I'm okay now."

She had no choice but to be okay. No choice but to deal or she'd have to live like Marie, bound in weepy, fragile grief. Dealing was saner. Accepting her anger and moving on the best she could was saner.

~*~

Matt now had a face for the ghost lurking between them. Whether knowing was worse or better, he was too unsettled to decide yet.

Jeb had been the image of the quintessential hero, a big, sturdy firefighter with his love for Katie shining in his face. He'd been the kind of man you'd want as a friend, as a neighbor . . .

As a husband for your best friend.

Matt's gut twisted, full of the sour burning pain he hadn't suffered in weeks. He replaced the album on the shelf and carted the box of notebooks downstairs.

Katie laid a hand over his before he could open the box. "Can we look at these later? I need some air. I'd like to go for a walk."

"Sure."

As they headed to the boardwalk, the images from Katie's wedding intruded on his usual enjoyment of their walks. She'd been so radiantly joyous in those photos. Yes, she laughed and smiled freely now, but his having seen the album revealed the changes left by her loss, the permanent strain and stain of grief's shadows.

How did he have a hope—

Enough! He wasn't competing with a dead man as he would with a living rival. Jeb was in the past, while he could give Katie a future. Maybe not what she originally dreamed, maybe not one-hundred percent of what she wanted, but he'd make sure she had everything in his power to provide. He would make this work.

They walked both ends of the boardwalk, scarcely speaking, but hand in hand, and when they reached her house after the long walk, enough ease had returned to Katie to make opening the box and reminiscing over an older, happier past simple.

The rambling, collaborative stories filling the old notebook pages were as clumsy and childish as he imagined, but they flooded him with good memories and chased back some of Katie's shadows. Soon they were sharing fresh elaborations and ideas, and laughing over one "Do you remember?" after another.

Laughter led to playful cuddles and teasing kisses and falling off the couch to more laughter and sizzling, mind-clearing lovemaking.

The next day was Saturday, and when Matt declared it a no-work day, Katie readily agreed. After an early breakfast, they fished off the dock, but caught only memories. They then headed up to the beach for a couple hours of sunning and swimming and on the walk home stopped for a lunch of pizza and ice cream.

Of course, being salty and sandy led to fooling around in the outdoor shower, deep kisses, and hurried, intense lovemaking under the streaming water, both of them fighting to keep quiet.

This was what he would do, just keep loving her, over and over. Erasing her past sorrows was beyond his power, but if he buried them under enough love and happiness in the now . . .

But that failed to solve the problem they faced with the future. He had career decisions ahead, and every moment with Katie deepened his rebellion against the approaching deadline.

He was debating whether they should put a movie on or a baseball game, when Katie's office phone rang.

She took one hesitant step away. "I should see who that—"

He didn't give her the chance for another step, but scooped her up in his arms and fell with her onto the sofa. "No work. They can leave a message." He kissed her hard and then teased her with light kisses until she was giggling again. He loved making her laugh.

He unwound the ponytail holder from her hair and dangled the frilly band in front of Katie.

"I've been meaning to ask—Don't get me wrong, you look amazing—but when did you go all girly? I remember you being a complete tomboy. And now, polished toes, dresses, flowers on your shoes, this—Fancy hair thing." He rattled the band embellished with twinkling beads until she snatched it away.

Katie giggled, her eyes sparkling, and she tossed the band onto the coffee table. "The makeover began about when I finally, finally got breasts. I was such a late bloomer. All my girlfriends were constantly going on about fashion and bras and boys, I went from clueless to longing to be a real girl. Monica and Desi dragged me over to the frilly side and I embraced the lace and pink with a passion."

He laughed, slipping his hand beneath her sleeveless turquoise blouse to cup her breast, caressing over the bra's thin lace. "I'm very happy about the chic lace undies. What color do we have today?"

He unbuttoned her blouse, one pearly button at a time, slowly revealing the bra and sweet curves of her breasts.

"Ah ha, baby pink today. Very pretty."

He slipped her blouse off her shoulders and away, and dipped his head to press kisses to her appealing, deep rose nipples tightening behind the lace.

She sighed blissfully and stretched back against the cushion.

He straightened, enjoying the bemused look in her eyes. Sinking his fingers into her damp hair, he combed through all the lovely curls and waves, rubbing fingertips over her scalp. He stroked lower and massaged the back of her head and neck.

"Oh, that feels so good." She relaxed into his hands with a sweet groan.

He took her mouth again, in no hurry, wanting this slow deep connection, breathing together, languidly lifting and riding together.

"Tell me what you want."

Her thoughtful smile sparked with amusement. "I want your shirt off."

"Yes, ma'am." He sat back and stripped off his T-shirt.

She raked her fingers through his chest hair, playing enticing patterns over his nipples, the sensation pleasantly blanking his mind.

"Katie . . ."

"You like that?" She repeated the motion.

He sucked in a sharp breath, very eager for more. "I like everything you do to me." He flopped onto his back. "I'm all yours for the taking."

"I'm so glad." She leaned over him, tantalizing his mouth with nibbles and licks, while her fingers danced lazy playful scratches and strokes across his chest. Her smile curled with sensual warmth. "Today I want play, nice and slow."

He stroked his hands over her soft skin. "I'm good with that plan." They could play all afternoon and into the night. Who needed movies?

With that, time for thinking and talking was over. Now was the time for another deep kiss, body to body, breathing together and sinking into the sweet relaxation, while time vanished and desire quietly fed the heat between them.

The rumble and crunch of a car pulling into Katie's driveway startled her out of their kiss.

She froze with her hands on his zipper. "Huh? Someone's in my driveway. I'm not expecting anyone today."

He stroked her arms, nudging her to finish freeing him from his shorts, desperate for the attention of her hands and mouth. "Probably just someone lost, turning around."

Normally reasonable, except their side of Bay Boulevard was one way only.

Katie wiggled free and leaned back, rosy, tousled, and tumbled from their kisses, listening with a puzzled face.

Cars doors shut.

"Someone's really here!" She snatched up her blouse and fumbled her arms into sleeves.

Rapping at the kitchen door, followed by the squeak of opening hinges jarred them into a scramble to straighten their clothing.

"Hello!" a woman warbled shrilly. "Kate, honey?"

Utter panic flooded Katie's pale face. "Oh, no, no. It's Marie, my mother-in-law." She gulped a breath and frantically clicked his waistband snap closed. "Put your shirt on, hurry! Oh, no. They never, never just pop in, not anymore. Hi, Marie. Be right there."

As mood killers went, this was a doozy.

As he yanked on his shirt, Katie pieced together a brittle smile and trudged toward the kitchen as if she were heading to a grim sentencing,.

"What a surprise! Hi, all. I thought we were getting together at your house on the eighth?" Katie managed a bright, welcoming tone for her guests.

"We had to drive down to Toms River, so we thought we'd swing by and say hello."

He followed into the kitchen. Katie had her hands locked tight behind her. The four people that had her all strung out latched eyes on him.

Jeb's parents appeared harmless, but Katie was too shaken to take chances. Beside the MacBains, Nadine fidgeted, fierce and fiery in the daylight, and Tony lurked uneasily in the rear, as if he dreaded what had Nadine fuming and Katie anxious.

Best to treat them all like potential hostile witnesses and take polite, firm charge. "Hi, good to see you again. Nadine, Tony. A pleasure to meet you, Mr. and Mrs. MacBain." He offered his hand. "Matt Powell."

Mr. MacBain automatically held out his hand. "Pleasure to meet you, too. Call me Daniel."

Daniel had a strong, welcoming grip. A beefy, ruddy man with a wide, friendly smile and a thin rim of rusty white hair circling his shiny scalp, he must have greatly resembled his dead son when he was a young man

His wife Marie was a soft, bottle-blonde woman who looked as if the slightest breeze could topple her. Her handshake was cool and fragile, but her icy blue gaze hinted she might be anything but weak. "We were so surprised when Nadine told us about you."

Matt grinned. "Our reunion was a happy surprise to us both."

"How about if you all get comfortable on the porch and I'll make drinks? Matt, would you help me?"

Nadine caught a hand on her mother's shoulder. "Sounds good. Mom, Dad, let's stop crowding the kitchen and take a seat."

Katie faced Matt, pleading filling her panicked eyes. "Please start the drinks, please? I have to run upstairs for a second."

"Sure."

Katie bolted for the stairs.

Matt turned. "What can I get everyone?"

Nadine clamped her lips in a strained smile. "I could definitely use a drink, thank you. Mom, Dad, what would you like?"

Mrs. MacBain continued scouring him with her stares. "Oh, my usual vodka and cranberry would be nice."

Nadine locked eyes on Matt as she firmly pressed her mother into motion toward the kitchen door. "I'd like a bourbon and soda. Thank you."

"Sounds good to me too." Mr. MacBain nodded happily, either ignoring or oblivious to his tension-filled family.

Matt nodded. "Got it. Tony, anything for you?"

"Just a ginger ale for me. Designated driver." He winced apologetically and followed his wife and in-laws.

"Sure." Matt set to pulling out glasses and the

liquor bottles.

Katie returned in a flash, still stressed and shaky, and rings sparkled on her left hand. She caught his glance and clenched her trembling hand. "I have to. While they're here, I *have* to."

She twisted the cap off the vodka bottle. "Nadine likes her drink strong and light on ice, but Daniel likes lots of ice. I'll take care of Marie's and Tony's. I should get the crackers and cheeses out, too. Marie likes the port wine cheese." She picked up the bottle, but her hand shook too much to pour.

Matt pulled the bottle from her hand. "Sweetheart, stop and take a breath. What's the problem here? How can I help?"

"Just help with the drinks. I'll explain later, after they go. They *never* just stop by. And we were, you know . . . I'm simply off balance. I'll be fine."

Chapter Eight

*O*H, SHE WAS SO NOT OKAY. KATIE GRABBED THE fresh box of assorted cocktail crackers and dumped them around the cheeses on the tray. What if they had walked in on her and Matt? They *always* called first. Why did they have to abandon habit and choose to be spontaneous, today of all days? Why not one quick call to give her at least a few minutes' warning?

Out on the porch, Matt calmly handed round the drinks, and everyone settled restlessly into their seats.

His brows rumpling, Daniel glanced sharply at his wife as if he'd been elbowed and then faced Matt over the rim of his glass with a shifting gaze. "Ah, so, I hear you and our Kate were friends when you were kids."

"My grandparents used to own the house next

door."

If only she could put on Matt's composed manner.

"We didn't know any Powell's." Marie gave him a suspicious glance-over.

"His grandparents were very good friends with my grandparents and parents for more than forty years. They sold and moved years before I met Jeb, Marie." She counted to five under her breath and offered out the cheese plate. "Won't you have some crackers?"

Matt shared the whole story of renting the place and rediscovering Katie after twenty years of missing her, amiably fielding Marie's querulous interruptions, staying light and upbeat, and carefully editing out their affair. He had a brilliant way with telling a story and controlling his audience. If he was this deft in court, building his case for a jury, she could appreciate why the three firms pursued him.

"Well, that was a fascinating story." Marie stood. "If you'll excuse me, I need to visit the bathroom."

As Marie left the porch, the impression of everyone releasing a heavy breath followed in her wake.

Katie took a deep sip of her drink. They showed no signs of being ready to head home, and it was late enough in the afternoon that she had no choice but to invite them to stay for supper. Her mind spun through what she had on hand to make an easy, filling meal for six. Spaghetti? Marie would complain about the carbs, but if she added in the chicken breasts in the freezer and a big salad—that would work. Cooking would give her a useful distraction from her stress.

At least Daniel, Nadine, and Tony appeared to like Matt. Marie was just difficult to please these days in any circumstance, but she wasn't a mean person, she was just not herself since Jeb died. Inconsolable grief warped everything.

"What have you done with Jeb's pictures?" Anguish filled Marie's screech.

She tottered into the doorway, hand clenching tight and white on the jamb, her lip trembling and watery eyes distraught as she nailed her gaze on Katie.

Oh, no, the photos! Katie's stomach rolled, and she cringed.

Normally she had some reasonable notice, giving her time to arrange the select pictures and replace the rings to continue the fiction, but this she'd been too startled out of her dreamy state from kissing Matt by her in-laws' arrival to think clearly and execute her routine. She'd at least remembered the rings, but setting out the photos . . . oh, this was going to be bad.

She opened her mouth, but nothing gelled in her tangled mind to say in her defense.

Nadine set her drink down with a sharp rap. "Cut it out, Mom, Kate's allowed to move on with her life. Jeb's been gone nearly four years. Yes, we miss him, but he's dead and buried and life goes on. Just because you've turned your house into a shrine to his memory, doesn't mean Kate has to."

As Katie shot Nadine a silent look of thanks, the simmering anger in Nadine's face directed at Marie took her aback.

Tears brimmed in Marie's eyes. "Jeb was a good man. I thought you loved him, Kate. Don't you love Jeb?"

I—I—Did. Don't. I hate him. I love him. He broke my heart!

But all those words jammed in Katie's throat.

Nadine rolled her eyes. "You need to face the truth, Mom. I loved my brother, but he was no saint. Jeb was a major jerk to Kate, and if he hadn't died first, she would have had every right to divorce him."

Katie froze. No, Nadine, no!

Daniel shifted uneasily in his seat, avoiding Katie's eyes.

Oh, no, did he know? If only she could run away . . .

Matt gently squeezed her shoulder, but the comfort was fleeting.

Unfortunately, Nadine was far from done.

"You know those 'nice girls' you met at the funeral? Well, they weren't Jeb's friends, they were his *girlfriends*, and no, they weren't from before he met Kate. You need to face facts, Mom. Jeb wouldn't have known what faithful meant even if you showed him in a dictionary. You always had blinders on for your perfect son. Some of us know the truth. He wasn't perfect at all. I don't blame Kate for taking off his rings and putting his pictures away. If I were her, I would have burned the photos and sold the damned rings."

"That's enough, Nadine." Daniel finally spoke up.

Tony tugged at Nadine arm. "Hon . . ."

"No, Dad, it's not!" She shook off Tony's hand.

"I loved Jeb, but he was an ass, a cheater, and he's dead and gone, and for sanity's sake we all need to move on. You need to let Kate move on and have a life. She's just been too sweet to tell you to back off and let her do what she needs to do for herself. I'm sick of you two keeping this fiction alive. And more, I'm sick of you expecting me to live up to a damned paragon who never existed."

Tears spilled from Marie's eyes. "Don't you talk that way about your brother! Don't you say such horrible lies! It's not true."

The rage Katie had never dared let loose exploded from Nadine. "It is true! My paragon of a brother cheated on Kate every chance he got. If it breathed and wore a skirt, he nailed it."

Katie sat paralyzed, speechless and unable even to breathe, hating the bafflement and pity filling Matt's face as Nadine's bitter outburst smashed her life's fragile balancing act.

~*~

Dumbfounded by the whole train wreck occurring in front of him, Matt stumbled for something to say or do that didn't involve tossing these damned people out on their ears.

Marie clutched the chair, shaking. "Stop it, Nadine, stop it! Why are you being so awful? He was a good boy. Kate, tell her she's wrong."

As Marie, Daniel, and Nadine bickered and ignored Tony's inept attempts to calm his wife and mother-in-law, Katie rose, pale face frozen in shellshock, took up her empty glass, and headed in the front door.

Anger at these people snapped Matt's resolve to keep the peace. He stood. "It would be best if you were gone when Katie comes back in." He nailed his glare on the miserable Tony. "Make sure they're gone."

He followed inside after Katie, but as he crossed through the living room, the kitchen door creaked and shut, followed by the clicking snap of the screen door.

Katie's empty glass sat on the counter, but no Katie. Where was she? He hurried through the kitchen door. No Katie on the side porch or on the back steps. Her car and the shower enclosure were empty. She hadn't headed south or north along Bay Boulevard. He rounded the corner. Not headed up to town either. Where had she run off to?

An old memory struck him, and he knew where she might have bolted. He jogged towards the bandstand, one of her hideouts of twenty years ago. Would she look there for refuge now?

A huddled flash of turquoise on the bayside steps confirmed his guess. He slowed his approach across the level stretch of sparse lawn.

Katie ignored him as he drew near, too wrapped in her harsh weeping. He sat beside her on the step without a word, needing to comfort her, but baffled as how to help. He wrapped his arm around her shaking shoulders and tucked her close. If only he had a handkerchief or tissue to give her.

She turning her face away, scrubbing a hand over her tears, but allowed his embrace.

He kept quiet. She'd talk when she was ready.

Shudders ran through her, her weeping slowed, and she sniffled now and then.

Seagulls wheeled above the docks, swooping low to check out the crabbers and soaring high in raucous squabbling aerobatics. Sails dotted the sparkling bright water. A man jogged past them across the grass with his dog bounding in puppyish strides.

"It's all true." She scrubbed her blouse hem over her face. "Jeb was unfaithful. A lot. I never knew until the funeral. His parents had no clue. I couldn't tell them. How could I?"

"I'm sorry. That must have been horrible."

"Those women, weeping over him, like they had a right to him. His fault. And they had the nerve to tell me . . . what . . . what they were to him. I trusted him. I never had a clue. How could I be so stupid?"

"Shit, I'm sorry, Katie."

"I hate him, and I miss him. I hate that he cheated on me. I hate that he died, and I hate that I can't change any of it. I'm, I'm, so . . . *angry*!" Her words ripped from her and she slugged his shoulder hard.

As if something had snapped in her with that sharp punch, she pounded him again in a fury, her eyes blind with tears.

"Katie, Katie—Stop! Calm down." Matt struggled to control her, but she got in numerous painful hits to his chest and shoulder.

Finally, he caught her wrists and pinned her against his body, immobilizing her as she fought him, shaking and sobbing her heart out. He hoped to hell and back nobody saw them and called the cops.

"Come on, Katie honey, you've got to calm down. Please."

Abruptly, she wilted into him, still sobbing, but all her fight extinguished. He eased up on his tight grip, but held her close. Her gasping sobs were breaking his heart.

Words finally emerged from her weeping. "He broke his promises. He promised me. Everyone breaks their promises." She swallowed and scrubbed at the fresh outpouring of tears.

"Not everyone." He patted her back.

Katie wrenched away, erupting in fresh, scalding anger. "Everyone! Even you! You promised to stay in touch. You promised me we'd be friends *forever*. You were my best friend in the world, and you just stopped!"

She tore loose from his arms and stumbled to her feet. "You left me!" she shouted, raw and broken.

Guilt stabbed him. He'd done exactly that.

"I was just a kid. *They* took me away! I was stupid kid, angry and hurt by my parents splitting up. I never meant to hurt you." He reached out.

She jerked back a step. "I was so stupid. I can't do this. You left me and you're going to leave me again."

"Katie, come and sit. I'm not leaving right away, and I'll be back. I'm never losing you again, I promise. I'm not that dumb ass kid anymore. Let's sit down and talk calmly."

"I can't. I just can't. I wrote to you and wrote to you, and you never wrote back." Her anger fizzled, and she slumped, her eyes hurt and lost. "I don't know what to trust anymore. I keep trusting the wrong things. You'd think I'd have learned by now, but, no, I keep hoping. I'm such a fool."

"You're not a fool. You're an intelligent, creative, loving woman."

"I haven't learned from my mistakes. I am so a fool. You're going to leave me again. I can't do that, not again."

"Loving someone with your whole heart doesn't make you a fool."

"Love's a mistake. A horrible mistake." She stepped back.

"No, Katie. Love's never a mistake. Your love, that's not a mistake. Letting love go is a mistake, treating love carelessly is a mistake. I was a dumb kid, and I made those mistakes, but I'm not a kid anymore. I'm not letting go. Come on, Katie, come sit with me. Catch your breath, and we'll talk."

She stared at him, stonily withholding even one shred of trust.

"Katie, our relationship is much more than some passing fling. We're far beyond just friends. I love you, and I know you love me."

~*~

Katie backed away. "I can't love you. I won't love you."

Oh, that's a lie.

Matt winced as if she'd slapped him, but simply held out his hand. "Come and sit until you're calmer."

Embarrassed and exhausted, she didn't know whom she was angry with anymore. She'd come so unglued. She'd *punched* Matt.

"I need to be alone. I need to go home."

"Just take a few more minutes."

"No." She trudged away shaking, trying to gather the shreds of her dignity. What if her in-laws were still at the house?

"Katie, please." Matt caught up to her, staying

her with a gentle hand on her shoulder.

She shrugged him off. "Leave me alone!"

Thankfully, Tony's SUV was gone. Breaking into a run across Bay Boulevard, she tore up her steps into the kitchen, spun around in a renewed panic and locked the door against Matt. She couldn't deal, just couldn't.

He jiggled the knob and knocked on the door. "Katie? Come on, please let me in."

No. She turned her back and ran to lock the front door. She'd learned her lesson. No more letting people just walk on into her house or into her life.

Ignoring his knocking and pleas to talk, she trudged upstairs into the bathroom to wash the salty burn from her aching eyes. Exhaustion dragged at her, and she paused, leaning on the sink, but her hands throbbed painfully.

What? She stared in puzzlement to find her knuckles were swollen and puffy. She'd hit Matt. She'd hit him hard enough to hurt her hands? Oh, no. Today was worse and worse.

Jeb's rings glittered at her. Enough. No more. This had to stop.

Slipping the rings off took cold water, lots of soap, and another bout of tears.

Maybe a bath would help. She started the tub filling, added a scoop of soothing bath salts to the water, and sat on the toilet to watch the water and thin froth rise.

The phone rang. The answering machine picked up.

"Hi, Katie, it's Mom. We'll be down bright and early tomorrow. Call me and let me know if you want us to bring anything special from the grocery on the way. Talk to you later."

No, she didn't want anything special. She wanted everyone to go away. She'd had it with everything.

Yes, she was simply having a tantrum because of emotional whiplash and exhaustion. Maybe she shouldn't be so surprised she'd finally lost her cool and broken down. Her fault for trying to shelter Marie. Her fault for trying to protect herself.

Maybe if she'd unleashed her grief fully at the time of hearing of Jeb's death and at the funeral, if she'd directed her anger at the guilty parties, at Jeb and his girlfriends, maybe the pain would be manageable today. The nasty, buried secret had boomeranged and clobbered her at the worst possible time.

If anything, today proved she wasn't ready for a new relationship.

Katie stripped and settled into the hot, deep water. Every bit of her ached like she'd had the flu. Her hands throbbed. She should have iced her hands instead of letting them float in the steamy water. Oh, how could she have hurt Matt? Squeezing her eyes shut against the fresh wave of humiliation, she rested her head against the bath pillow.

The phone rang again. "It's Nadine. Katie, I'm sorry. I never meant to let it blow out like that. I screwed up. I'm so, so sorry. I'm sick to death of Mom's denial, we were already fighting before we got to your house, but that's no excuse for what I did. I'm sorry. I'm sorry."

More tears leaked.

Oh, shouldn't she be cried out by now?

Shutting her eyes, she focused on simply breathing and allowing her mind to go blank

The phone ringing jolted her awake. The water was cold, and she was pruney.

Matt's calm, stern voice came over the answering machine. "Katie, we need to talk. I love you. Pick up the phone, please."

No, not tonight. She'd fall completely apart if she talked to anyone, especially Matt.

If she had any sense, she'd just let him leave without ever talking to him again. If she gave in and let him talk, he'd just confuse her with desire again, and she'd once again make a stupid decision based on emotions.

Chapter Nine

*A*FTER A CRAPPY, MOSTLY SLEEPLESS NIGHT, MATT hit the bakery early, determined to get over to Katie's armed with breakfast and reason and tackle yesterday's mess and the discussion of their future before her parents arrived. Sitting down with the comforts of coffee and food always aided negotiations.

He ended up buying far too many pastries, but he picked all her favorites and a loaf of country white bread as well, in case she wanted something plain.

His heart jammed in his throat as he knocked on her kitchen door. He shrugged his tight shoulders and the pain in his neck stabbed miserably. The bruises Katie had given him didn't help matters. As for his stomach, well, shit. Despite the pills, his stomach was killing him, and he held little hope eating would help. His earlier mug of coffee on an empty stomach had proved a bad move, but he'd been desperate for the caffeine.

Katie peeked through the curtains, and her long pause before unlocking the door ramped up his tension. She barred his approach in the doorway, clutching her thin bathrobe close, and her eyes were puffy, shadowed, and wary.

"I brought breakfast." He held up the bags. "A little of everything."

"I'm not hungry."

"You can share the extras with your parents. Did you make your coffee yet?"

Katie shook her head.

He stepped forward. "Have a seat, and I'll make you your coffee."

With a shrug, she gave way and allowed him in. She sat at the table, sad and rumpled

Matt busied himself with the coffeemaker, loaded the pastries onto a platter, sliced the bread, and set out the butter and jam. Yeah, he'd overdone the food.

She chose a crumb bun, but settled back into her seat without eating.

He fixed their coffees. His soft caress to her shoulder as set her mug in front of her received a stiffening of her back.

Right. Of course, why would any of this be easy?

He sat across from her and selected a piece of bread, hoping the simple slice would soak up and subdue the nasty combination of stomach acid and coffee already fighting in his gut.

"Katie, I wish I knew a way to make this all

better. I wish I could go back in time and never be that stupid kid who hurt you. I wish I had kept you in my life. I don't know how to apologize enough for failing you then. All I can say is I'm sorry."

She dropped her gaze. "I know."

"But that's the past. We've found each other again. We have something great together. I know we can make this relationship work. I have to leave on Friday, but I'll be back. I have to square away the sale of my house and get the move set."

"I know. Did you decide which firm?" Still avoiding his eyes, she picked at the crumbs, chipping them off the bun and leaving them uneaten on the plate.

"No, not yet. As I mentioned, the decision's difficult. They're all excellent firms, any one of them will position me where I want to be on my career path, but I'm still weighing the options carefully."

"If they were right for you, you'd know. You'd have already decided."

"I'm just being sensible and cautious. Moreover, now there's us together to consider. That's seriously changed how I'm analyzing my choices. Working with Bernard Harding is extremely tempting, but Atlanta's so far from you. D.C. would be better. Wherever I end up, location won't stop us from being together."

She shook her head. "No. You'll promise to stay in touch, and you will for a while, and you'll come visit when you can, but you know you'll be swept up into the work. The job will take all of your attention and energy. You'll be taking on important cases, you'll be settling in, you'll need to focus on work. That's what you want. That's what you need.

You know it. You've told me."

Had he said that? That didn't sound like what he'd said, but maybe that's what she'd heard.

"Katie, I'm not that dumb kid anymore. This isn't a passing fling we have here. Having you in my life is essential. If I choose D.C., I'll be in driving distance. Heck, I can take the train. We'll see each other often. Even if I choose Richmond, we can make this work."

"If, if, if. What if you choose Atlanta? And tell me again, at your old firm, how often did you actually take time away from the job? Almost never, you told me."

"That's one of many reasons why I quit. That's one of many reasons why I want one of these partnerships. I'll be able to make time."

"You know that's not how it will be. You know you'll be targeting that next goal beyond the partnership. A long distance relationship is too hard to maintain. You'll meet new people. I want you to put your full focus and energy into reaching every goal in your career."

Icy fear crawled his spine. She was saying goodbye. No! He refused to accept that outcome.

"I swear it, Katie. I keep my promises. We will make this work. We have all week to work out the details. This decision is no longer just my choice about my career. I want your input on where I'm going, because I want you there with me. I want you to come live with me."

"No." Tears ran over her cheeks, and she pushed away from the table. "I can't deal with this. I need you to go before Mom and Dad get here. I need time to calm down. I need you to go."

He stood reluctantly, wanting to be agreeable and aching for her pain, but also wanting to finish this discussion. His stomach tightened into a burning knot. His instincts screamed for him to hold his ground. Walking out her door now would be a mistake.

Only, she was too exhausted and too emotional to be receptive. Once she'd calmed, once she'd rested, then they could discuss matters productively and work out their plans.

"Okay. We still need to finish this talk, but I'll give you space while your parents are here. Then, after they go home, I'll come over." The alarm in his heart roared *Stay!* but concern for her forced him to step out the door into the morning sunshine. "I'll see you in a bit."

She stared at him, her expression wooden. "No. Don't come back. Our being together was a mistake. I'm sorry. I can't do this." She shut the door between them and clicked the lock.

"Katie! We are not done discussing this."

She just shook her head and turned away. "I need to be alone. Please, just go away. Goodbye."

The burst of anger and helplessness smashed the last of his willpower. Even as he knew losing his cool could only make things worse, he lost it, pounding on the door.

"Katie, this isn't the way. We can make this work. Please, Katie. I love you. Just talk to me, I don't want to lose you again." He banged again. "Katie, please. Don't do this to us."

He was talking to an empty kitchen.

Gutted, he trudged down the steps, retracing the old familiar path over to his place.

No, this wasn't his place. This wasn't even Nana and Pop's anymore. The rental was just a building. He needed to stop pretending he belonged here. He didn't. Never would. Katie had made that clear.

Anger surged back over his depression. Was he just going to limp off in defeat?

Hell, no. He wouldn't let them end like this.

~*~

She'd ruined everything with Matt.

Katie sagged against the kitchen wall, hands knotted to keep from opening the door. Matt's heartrending groan and his footsteps leading off the porch shattered her, but letting him back in would be a horrible mistake for them both.

With a sob, she ran upstairs, stripped, and threw herself into the shower to drown her crying.

Stop this! Pull yourself together. You're an adult. You're allowed to decide if and when you want a relationship and with whom. You're allowed to end a relationship that will fail. End this before you hurt any worse.

Only, the pain on Matt's face was killing her, and she'd deliberately put that pain there.

But he'd said he loved her. What if he did really love her?

Oh, really, what does saying I love you matter? Jeb said he loved you, and he still broke your heart. You have to protect yourself.

Right. She couldn't give her heart away again until she was utterly safe and sure.

This thing she and Matt had couldn't last under the strain of his career. Here, he was on vacation, feeling the freedom from having quit an onerous job, one that he'd thrown his heart and soul into despite the aggravations and intense stress. The way he'd talked about his work, he loved his career. Now that he had his pick of dream firms? He'd throw himself into the work with relish.

Matt had been that way as a boy, totally involved in whatever project they were doing. He was always getting in trouble for arriving home late because he'd been too focused on an activity. He'd lose himself in writing up his stories or work until he was exhausted to learn a new trick on his skateboard or on the boogie board.

Since Matt didn't know the meaning of quit, she had to put a stop to this lost cause of a relationship for him and free him to pursue his dreams.

Waterlogged and miserable, she pried herself from the shower. A glance at the clock surprised her at the time. Her parents would be here all too soon. She needed pull her act together before they arrived.

Katie dressed and dragged downstairs. She wrapped the pastries and bread, dumped her tepid coffee, and poured a new cup, but the fresh coffee sloshed acidly in her empty stomach. She choked down the bun and dumped the crumbs in the trash.

In an attempt to distract her thoughts, she planted herself in front of the computer. She should have called her parents and told them to stay home.

Unfortunately, the routine of work failed to shut down the storm of guilt, sorrow, anger, and pain. She hadn't cried like this since Jeb's death. Made sense, this was a death of another relationship—except she was the one killing it this time. Cutting Matt off hurt horribly, but was necessary. She'd survived the heartbreak of Matt disappearing from her life once before, she would survive this time too.

She dreaded facing another lingering, long distance end. Quick and final was best.

Mom and Dad rushed in all frazzled with worry.

"Why's the door locked? Why didn't you answer your phone? Nadine called us this morning. She's so worried about you. Oh, honey, you've been crying."

A fresh flood of tears spilled, as if she hadn't already cried a river.

Mom rocked Katie in her arms. "Oh, baby. I thought Matt would be here with you. Nadine said he was with you."

"He's not. I sent him away."

"Aw, honey. Why do you always go making things so hard on yourself?"

If only she knew.

"We won't be seeing each other anymore."

"Why on earth? Katie, what's going on here? You were so happy to be friends again."

"He's leaving. It's just too hard. There are too many years between us. We had fun, but, but . . ."

A hot swell of tears burned at her eyes and clogged her throat. She'd been *happy*.

"That boy loves you, honey."

"We won't be able to make it work. He has this grand career ahead. No room for more. We talked, and he thinks he loves me, but it's too complicated, and I can't deal with complicated. I want my simple life. I'm not ready for more."

"I doubt that very much. You're just overwrought. I bet you barely slept and only had coffee for breakfast."

Mom bustled, fussed, and scolded. Dad

threatened to head next door to talk to Matt and straighten out this whole mess.

"You're making a big mistake. If he takes the job in Atlanta, you can just move to Atlanta. Don't think you have to stick here in Jersey with us. If being with Matt makes you happy, for heaven's sake, be with him."

"We've only known each other for nine days."

"Nonsense, you've known him forever."

"Forever minus the last twenty years. That missing time period's kind of important. I knew a boy. I don't know him as a man at all."

Dad covered her hand in a consoling squeeze. "Matt's the same boy you've always known. Anyone could see the truth of that just looking at him. You can tell deep down he's the Matt you knew."

Shaking her head, Mom headed to the fridge and pulled out the carton of eggs. "You need to work this out with Matt, dear. A friendship like you two have is too important to lose. If Matt loves you and you love him, don't let things that went wrong with Jeb push you into making a foolish mistake. You've been holding people off for four years, don't push Matt away too."

Mom made her eat, and they both drove her nuts, and she fought with them, but she stood firm on her decision.

It was for the best.

~*~

"Please, Katie, just pick up and talk to me. We can work this out—"

Her answering machine cut him off.

Matt hung up, squashing the urge to charge next

door and pound on her door until she let him in. Except, despite his resolve he found himself heading out the door. He grabbed onto the post and dropped onto the steps, utterly drained and scoured clean of hope.

He'd failed. For the first time, he'd failed to win the goal he'd set his mind to.

How could Katie doubt he'd keep his promises? He was nothing like Jeb.

Fury rose. How dare she lump him in with men like his dad and Jeb when he'd done nothing to deserve her lack of trust! He *never* went back on his word or cheated on a girlfriend and he despised those men who did. Katie once believed in the best of everyone. How had she given up on trusting him?

No, he'd failed badly before this. He'd failed with his parents, too. So many years of struggling to get them to notice him, to be proud of him, to prove he meant more to them than a possession in the unending custody and support battles. Nothing he did was ever enough.

Apparently, his best wasn't enough for Katie either.

His stomach wrenched. Suddenly, all the prestige he'd fought for that should have given him happiness, was flat and worthless. He'd finally discovered the real prize he'd wanted in his life— and she didn't want him.

He shoved up from the step and headed off hard away from their block. If he stayed here, without a doubt he'd do something stupid, like pound on her door again or fall on his knees and beg.

He ended up at the Seaward Inn bar with a

vodka martini in front of him. Drinking solved nothing, but numbing the pain for a couple hours would be a relief and keep him away from the phone and her door. Both of them needed to cool off and have some space.

Except, holding the icy martini glass between his hands just sank him into memories of their night here and kiss on the boardwalk. That pure, perfect kiss before either of them had let reality interfere.

Giving up infuriated him, but maybe bowing out was for the best. This had all been crazy and fast, and he'd been in deep before he'd thought anything through.

But . . . being with Katie was the best thing in his life. How could he just walk away?

He ordered a steak and second drink. Somehow, he'd find the solution.

All around him, couples filled the tables, old, young, happy, unhappy, but the elderly couple in the corner table caught his particular attention. They had to have been together for forever and you could just tell they were happy as they talked together. Love shone in their faces as if they were twenty instead of pushing eighty. He could see himself being happy like that with Katie, talking about their kids and grandkids and smiling at each other with love in their eyes.

Letting Katie run and shut him out as he'd shut her out when they were kids was beyond wrong. She was simply scared, but how would he reach past those fears to convince her they had a relationship worth the risks?

He chuckled. He'd forgotten Katie's stubborn side. Remembering how sweet and fun she'd been and closing his eyes to the streak of obstinacy that had occasionally landed them both in trouble was far simpler.

Since giving up was unacceptable, he needed a plan.

However, time was running out. His rental was up in four days, and extending his stay was impossible. He'd already checked, and the house was booked solid through the end of the season.

As he slowly finished his meal and drink, his mind churned on fruitlessly.

He needed to make a decision on the firms, but none of them appealed any longer. Katie had jumbled all his priorities.

Actually, his priorities had completely transformed.

However, he still had to give an answer to one of them.

He pushed away his empty plate and waved to the bartender for another drink.

Did he? What rule mandated he must say yes to any of them? Time for some serious rethinking and decisions.

If he were honest with himself, he'd lost enjoyment in his career. While he had been looking forward to the new challenges, prestige, and superior income in the current offers, he'd been dreading the inevitable grind of the work.

Did you ever consider that this is probably the real reason you've been unwilling to commit to a decision before now? Did you ever consider that maybe it's a sign to bail on being an attorney?

Boggled at that out-of-the-blue thought, his mind freewheeled along on the alcohol buzz.

Give up his career? He'd be insane to turn down all the offers. He'd worked too damned hard to falter now. He had what it took to excel in his career. He'd given up trying to impress Dad long ago. He was the one who wanted this career move.

Damn, then what's with all this whining? Just shut up with this poor me shit and make your choice.

That didn't change the fact that his accomplishments now felt flat and stale. That didn't change the fact that a likely bleak future lurked behind his glossy choices.

Only, wait just a minute—

Couldn't he have another option beyond the three firms or quitting entirely? He wanted to be here, building a future with Katie. That empty storefront wandered into his mind. He could open his own office, here, in New Jersey. He could stay here, with Katie, in the place they both loved.

No . . . He shook his head. Shifting his practice to a non-reciprocating state like New Jersey would be an annoying, time-consuming set of hoop-jumping steps. He'd be starting his career over practically at zero. No clients. No connections. The time delay . . . That would be really crazy, right?

Finished with the third drink, he cut himself off and paid his tab.

Well, that timeout had used up several hours and solved nothing. He headed to the crosswalk, but paused dizzily at the corner.

Okay, maybe he should head to the boardwalk and walk off some of this buzz before he attempted crossing any streets.

Only, walking the boardwalk came with too many memories. He took the first pavilion entrance to the beach, but negotiating the stairs in the dark rubbed in his level of inebriation. He walked down to the waterline, skirting the dark, rushing tide and pale foam rolling up and sweeping away. A wave caught him, surging around his calves and soaking his sandals and pants.

He stumbled back until he reached dry sand and sat, arms folded on knees and chin on arms. He shut his eyes, drifting on the ocean's tireless roar and rumble mixed with the alcohol's buzz, and surrendered to bittersweet reminiscing.

Soft laughter dragged him into the present, and he opened his eyes. A couple walked past along the wet firm sand, arm in arm, pausing to kiss between dodging the dark sweep of tide and foam. His heart wrenched.

Drunk and maudlin. Way to go.

Time to stop banging against this setback like some stupid moth fighting to reach a light bulb. He was smarter than this. Didn't his degrees prove he was smarter than a moth? Yeah, so he'd better start thinking like the bright, hotshot attorney everyone claimed he was, and find a fresh solution. A solution always existed, often far from obvious, but there was always a way to win and settle a case.

Step one: For tonight, quit feeling sorry for himself and get some sleep.

Step two: Tomorrow, revise attitude, list options, and make decisions around the priority of winning back Katie.

Chapter Ten

*K*ATIE TUCKED THE VACUUM CLEANER INTO THE closet. The springy hose slipped and knocked the can of spray paint off the shelf with a clatter. She tucked the partially used can back on the shelf. Maybe she should purge the closet. Going on a three-day house-cleaning binge had done little to help except exhaust her so she could sleep, and the house practically sparkled.

The mail should be here. She peeked out the front window. Good, the coast was clear, Matt's car was missing, and . . .

The house looked closed up.

No! A wrenching pang knocked the relief right out of her. It was only Thursday! He wasn't supposed to leave until tomorrow! What if he'd already left for good?

Serves you right. That's what you wanted. You sent

him away. What's done is done. Now you have to deal.

She had. She did.

Oh, she'd made such a mess of everything.

Sick to death of crying, she clenched her throat against the newest dull throb of tears and forced herself outside.

An armload of mail filled the box today. Katie squinted against the bright morning sunshine, sorting through the pieces. Still so much junk mail arrived in Jeb's name, the catalogues that wouldn't stay cancelled, charity letters . . .

MacBain. MacBain. MacBain—

She banged the hatch closed.

The name still filled her sight in bold calligraphy flowing across the mailbox's beautifully painted shore scene. *MacBain.*

"Damn you, Jeb!"

Pain, anger, and grief slammed her like icy knives, shattering the numb shell she'd lived in for the last four years and that she'd carefully repaired over the past several days.

No more! Time to stop aiding and enabling the lie.

She tore into the kitchen and threw the mail at the table, indifferent to the envelopes and flyers skittering off the polished wood to the floor. She flung open the closet, grabbed the spray paint, and sprinted outside, shaking the can furiously.

Gritting her teeth, she aimed at the M and pressed the button.

Gasping, uneven lavender gouts spurted and spritzed over the navy blue letters, thin and hazy in spots and dripping down to the sand in others. The spray died after Mac and part of the B, leaving only lavender-spotted Pain.

Oh, what a mess, what a splotchy, hideous mess!

Tears spilled. Guilt twisted and chilled. She'd ruined Marie's lovely painting, just like Jeb's cheating had ruined the picture of their happy marriage.

Stop! Time to stop. Time to do this right.

She gulped for breath, scrubbing her hands over her tears, and headed inside on shaky legs.

No more living in limbo. She found an empty box in the attic and went around the house, filling the box with all the framed pictures of Jeb, but she set their vacation photo albums on the shelf with the wedding album. Completely erasing her past with Jeb felt wrong, so she'd decide how to handle the albums at another time. A strange, easing calm filled her heart as she carted the box out to her car.

Next, she called Nadine at work and walked upstairs as she patiently waited to be transferred.

Nadine picked up the call, her voice cautious. "Hi, Kate. How are you doing?"

"Better than this weekend. I know it's last minute, but can we meet for lunch today?"

"Yes! I don't have any meetings."

"How about Flynn's Grill at noon?"

"I'll be there. And, Kate, I'm truly sorry."

"I know. Me too. It's going to be okay. We'll talk at lunch."

After showering and dressing, she tucked the box containing her wedding band and engagement ring in her purse.

First, she headed to the home improvement store, where she bought a new white mailbox and bright brass stick-on house numbers.

Next, she stopped at the jewelers and left lightened of two rings, but wearing a new gold charm bracelet with one twinkling gold and diamond star charm. She'd fill the bracelet with her dreams.

When Katie arrived at the restaurant, Nadine was waiting on the bench outside, her face somber. She leapt up with jittery energy and threw her arms around Katie. "I'm sorry, I'm sorry, I don't want to lose being friends with you. I was so out of line on Saturday."

Katie squeezed her tightly. "I'm sorry, too. I don't want to lose being friends with you either. Looking back, I'm amazed this all didn't blow up sooner. Let's go in and talk over wine and food. I'm hungry for the first time in days."

They both settled on steak and a bottle of Cabernet Sauvignon.

"That's a beautiful bracelet. It's new?" Nadine reached across the table and ran a finger over the ornate links and charm.

Katie took a swallow of wine and a deep breath and met Nadine's eyes. "I traded in Jeb's rings."

Nadine nodded firmly. "Good for you."

"You approve?"

"It's not up to me to approve or disapprove. It's what you needed to do for you. How do you feel about the decision?"

"Good. Free."

"Then you did the right thing."

"I loved Jeb."

"I know you did."

"I've been so angry and lost. I thought I was

doing okay, but I really haven't been. What I was doing wasn't healthy for any of us."

Nadine clasped Katie's hands. "I'm sorry. We all should have helped, and we only made it harder."

"I need a favor. I have a box of photos in the car. I need you to take them for now."

"Okay."

"I'm not erasing Jeb from my life. I don't want to hurt your mom. However, I can't go on like we were. I need to make changes and find some healthy balance."

"I understand. Mom's agreed to talk to our pastor about grief counseling. It's a start."

"I'm glad."

She should probably look into some counseling for herself. She was far better than she'd been, but getting outside advice on how to balance Jeb's place in her life might be a good decision.

"And Matt?" Nadine glanced over the rim of her glass.

Katie sighed, the new burning behind her eyes threatening her teetering composure. "That's over. I think he's already gone."

Nadine shook her head, regret filling her face. "Aw, Kate. I'm sorry. I messed that up for you. I thought you and he were good together. Tony liked him."

"You didn't mess us up. I did."

Even if letting Matt go was the right decision in the long run, she should have handled saying goodbye a hundred times better.

She fought the ache in her heart. "Chalk that up to summer madness and a failed experiment to make more out of an old friendship that wasn't meant to be. I ended up last in a relationship once already. I don't want to fall into the same mistake again. We'll stay in touch, I'm sure, but we want different things out of life. He's headed for a stellar career, but work will consume his time. I wouldn't be surprised to see him become a judge or senator in the future. Heck, President. Wouldn't that be fun to see him in the news someday and say I knew him when?"

And would this unending ache for him still be there then?

Nadine frowned thoughtfully. "I know I don't know Matt like you do, but he didn't strike me as the kind of man who would put you last in his life."

"Purely the illusion of vacation. He wouldn't do it purposefully, but he's admitted he throws himself fully into his work, that his hectic career left no room for a personal life, and I can't see that changing at any of the new firms. Wherever he chooses to go, life will be all forward charge for Matt, ever onward and upwards."

"I don't know. Matt seemed very into you. He's not my brother. Jeb was a good-hearted, fun-loving guy—yes, he had lots of great qualities, and I know he did love you—but he was also too often unfocused, thoughtless, and immature."

"Matt's kind of the complete opposite." Too serious, too dedicated.

Nadine handed her a warm roll. "Drink your wine and tell me about Matt. I told the office I had a family emergency. I have all afternoon, and Tony can deal with the kids if we need longer. Tell me how you first met. Tell me everything."

Katie sipped her wine, but swallowing was

difficult under the wash of precious memories and the lump of emotion tightening her throat. She sighed.

"We were eight and for five years he was my best friend in the world. I never really understood back then, but I loved him from the start. I was playing over at the kids' beach on the merry-go-round . . ."

Her story poured out all through their meal and more wine, tears, tissues, and laughter. Nadine pushed her through every memory, from Matt's first cocky *"You're not big enough,"* to this morning and the pain at seeing his empty driveway.

She never imagined she'd held so much inside of her and when she was finally finished, she felt empty and adrift, like the breaking of a fever after the flu.

Nadine locked eyes on her. "You know you have to fix this. You love him."

Katie twisted her wineglass between her fingers. "I don't know if I can. Or should."

Letting him go was killing her, but he had lofty dreams for his future. He needed to be free to seize those dreams. More hot tears rolled over her cheeks.

"You're strong enough, and you should." Nadine shoved more tissues into her hands. "I just have one last question. Answer me simply yes or no."

Her momentous pause sent Katie's mind spinning on what she could possibly ask.

Nadine leaned forward on her elbows, her blue eyes sharp and focused. "Do you love Matt? Yes or no?"

Katie's "Yes!" cracked out of her before she

could edit her thoughts.

Nadine grinned. "There's your answer. Don't let Matt go."

~*~

Keeping his distance when Katie was only yards away was killing Matt, however his gut told him space and patience was the right course for the moment. Back when they were kids, after any quarrel with her siblings or cousins, she'd always needed to withdraw from everything and cool down for a bit. His memories and gut had better be right.

By Thursday evening, Matt had the final pieces of his plan in place. Maybe a crazy plan, but the time had come to throw a Hail Mary pass and see what happened. If that failed, he was getting a room in the nearest motel and implementing Plan B.

Friday morning arrived. Matt finished the last cup of coffee from the old percolator and took a deep breath. His two weeks were up. Despite his current turmoil, staying here had been a good decision.

Final packing up and cleaning took only minutes. Taking a seat at the kitchen table, he glanced at the clock.

Time to put things in motion.

He made his first two calls. Turning down the offers was easy and smooth on his end. The head partners were unhappy with the news, but he had nothing personal invested with either firm other than respecting the men and appreciating their offers.

His third call was the hard one. "Bernard Harding, please. It's Matthew Powell. Mr. Harding is expecting my call. Thank you."

He sucked in a stiff breath. No going back after this call. He'd liked Bernard right off and hated disappointing the man, but he had new goals.

"Matthew! I've been looking forward to hearing from you. Do I have good news to share with Sam and Xavier?"

"I want to thank you all for the extremely tempting offer."

Bernard sighed. "I hear a 'but' coming."

"This has been a difficult decision, but unexpected changes in my personal life have complicated matters."

"You're turning us down."

"I need to relocate to New Jersey. Katie—" He cut himself off. Bernard didn't need the whole story like Katie did.

Bernard chuckled. "Are congratulations in order? I'm real sorry you won't be joining us, but I wish you all the best, and if you're ever in Atlanta I expect you to call me, and we'll meet for that golf rematch."

"It's a deal."

He finished the call with honest regret. He would have learned a lot working with Bernard, but at least he hadn't burned his bridges.

Done. Holy shit, he'd done it!

He waited for the expected queasy grind and bite of his stomach. Nothing.

Feeling lightheaded, he shoved to his feet and slipped the phone in his pocket. Dizzy? No, he was less lightheaded than *lightened*. No doubts. He'd made the right choice stepping off the fast track.

Okay, past and present all attended to. Time to work on his future.

He loaded the cooler and laptop into the trunk and locked the door for the last time. Lightning flashed over the bay under a darkening, stormy sky, and distant thunder rumbled.

He laughed. Hopefully that wasn't an omen.

Let's do this.

Heart lodged in his throat, he backed the car into the street and immediately swung into Katie's driveway and parked beside her car.

Nothing about Katie and he being together was a mistake. The mistake he'd made over the past several days was trying logic, when the answer was following his heart. There was nothing logical about being in love. Nothing timely, rational or organized about love.

Raindrops pattered, and the breeze gusted as he popped the trunk. He slung his laptop and carry-on bag straps over his shoulder, grabbed the cooler, and headed for her front door. He knocked and held his breath.

Please open the door. Please.

Katie opened the door so quickly, she must have been there watching. "What's wrong?"

His hopes intensifying, he gently barged past her with the next gust of wind. "A few things. First off, I figured why waste the leftover food and wine when you could use them."

Mission Step One accomplished. He was inside her house.

She blinked. "Uh, sure, okay. Thanks."

He set the cooler on the kitchen counter. While Katie was distracted with sorting food into her full, orderly fridge, he let his two bags softly slide to the floor.

Finished organizing, she turned to him, puzzlement in her eyes. "What else?"

"This." He scooped her into his arms and into the kiss he'd needed to take and give all these last frustrating days.

She stiffened, and for a heart-stopping moment, he feared he'd guessed wrong.

Then she melted into him with a shivering groan, joining in the kiss. She tasted of lemon and sweet tea. Her damp, freshly-washed hair held the scent of flowers and citrus.

With Katie in his arms, the grinding, empty ache in his chest vanished. Feeling complete again, he caught her up off her feet.

Startled, she gasped and clutched at his shoulders, but stayed in the kiss and wrapped her legs around his waist.

He headed toward the staircase. Navigating the steps while locked in their kiss proved an interesting, awkward exercise, but they arrived in her bedroom without incident.

He gently lowered her to the bed.

Katie scrambled to her knees and pressed a hand to his chest, breathing hard. Her eyes were dazed and wild.

"Stop. Wait! Wait. I need to think. We have to talk!"

Talk? Now? Chuckling, he toed off his shoes. "I've been trying to talk with you for the last four days."

"I know, but—"

He cut her off with a fierce kiss, determined to keep her from thinking about anything but the love he knew they shared, needing to convince her to believe.

"But, but . . ." She softened again, her hands caught his shoulders, and she deepened the slow consuming kiss.

With another prayer, he poured her with all the love and hope in his being into that kiss.

Unfortunately, the necessity for them both to break loose in order to breathe again allowed her time to think.

She wriggled free, panting and her face flushed, and scuttled backwards into the mounded pillows against the headboard. "You need to let me think!"

"I figured out our problem. Too much talking. Too much thinking. Not enough kissing. Not enough loving."

He caught her ankle, stroking a thumb over her soft skin as he considered a playful tug to draw her back into his arms, but released his grip and knelt in front of her, sitting back on his heels.

Eyes wide and dark, Katie tucked up her knees, but stayed defensively huddled in place, when she could have escaped the bed. A variety of thoughts flickered over her expressive face and her gaze drifted to where he was all too achingly confined in his shorts.

He swallowed a groan.

Her tongue delicately moistened her lips, and then, as if she'd realized her drifting attention, she snatched her gaze back to his face and tensely bit her plump lower lip.

"We can't do this."

Matt smiled. "We can, we should, and we need to." He fished the ring from his pocket. "Because I love you, and I know you love me."

Her gaze caught on the ring. A gasp escaped her, and she trembled, her face stunned.

Here goes everything. He locked his eyes on her and offered out the ring. "Katie, will you marry me?"

Tears spilled over Katie's cheeks.

In her silence, he kept brushing and kissing each tear away, scared as he'd never been before that she didn't want a future together, that she was unable to leave her grief and pain behind.

If she said no . . . He'd have to carry on without her, and the possibility ripped pain through him worse than his worst heartburn.

Please oh, please, Katie, take on this new life with me, be in it with me. He dragged in a wrenching breath.

"I'm not leaving you again. Please, give me a chance. Give us a chance. Wear my ring, be my sweet Katie."

~*~

How was this happening?

Katie fought the rattling shakes. Matt was *leaving*. He was moving to Washington, D.C., or Richmond, or Atlanta. She'd *told* him to go. She'd told him he needed to follow his dream.

But here he was with a ring and an earnest face and this baffling claim that he was staying . . .

Breathless and dazed with disbelief and hope, she shook her head. "Marry? This is too fast. Our lives are too different." She snapped her mouth closed on her babbling. She wanted him to have his dream, but she wanted him. She wanted so much, too much.

"I know this all seems fast, but not really. We've

known each other forever."

"But, but, how can you stay here? The partnership you're taking, your career . . ."

"I turned down all three offers."

Her mouth dropped open. What? Why? He'd worked too hard to abandon the brilliant career ahead of him. "Are you crazy?"

He laughed. "Brightman and Clancy both politely suggested maybe I'd gone way round the bend, but I don't think I've been saner. Bernard wished me luck. I've learned so much in the last two weeks that I've been utterly blind to over the last two decades. I've been working my ass off all my life, futilely trying to win Dad's approval even after he died. Straight A's didn't bring Dad back. Valedictorian didn't satisfy. Getting into Stanford Law — nothing. Every last target I strove for, I reached, I won, I *earned*. Only, the prizes have proved more fool's gold than treasure. I was missing two very important items in my life. I didn't have love, and I wasn't happy. I want to be happy, Katie. I want love. I want to come home to something more than exhaustion, briefs to read, and an empty house."

"But what will you do?"

"That vacant shop we saw got me to thinking. I could open my own office. Hell, Nadine mentioned that her non-profit was looking to hire an affordable in-house counsel."

"Work for Nadine! You definitely are crazy!"

"Crazy for you. When I walked out of McCollister, Janowitz, and DiTommaso, I thought I'd solved all my problems, but I hadn't thought far enough through the issues, and I nearly charged straight into the same old trap, just a glossier, ego-polishing, well-paid trap. I quit MJD's because I was burned-out, I was hating the man I saw in the mirror, and I saw myself heading for the same empty, workaholic life and early heart attack as my dad. I took a hard look my future, and I hated everything I saw."

Matt nailed her with passionate eyes. "Being with you again reminded me that I used to have dreams. Good ones. Remember all the stuff we used to dream about together? Working myself to death in a lonely life wasn't any part of those dreams. Now, most of those were childish stuff, true, but I want to make new dreams with you. I want to dream with you again. Do you want to share our dreams again?"

She shook her head, as shaky and off-balance as if she were scrambling over cracking, slippery ice. "You can't decide to marry someone after only two weeks! I made such a mistake before. I can't rush into another mistake."

"I'm so sorry Jeb let you down, but I'm not that guy. I'm also not a hurt, angry boy anymore. When I make a promise now, I keep it. Us together isn't a mistake. As for deciding I want to marry you? I basically knew you've *always* been the one for me since my first day back here, although admitting the truth to myself did take me a little longer. I've loved you since I first saw you pushing the merry-go-round."

He leaned forward and kissed her. "I saw a girl who didn't give up on a challenge. So, let me hear you love me. I know you do. If you love me, then together we can make everything work, no matter what. I want to make a life with you, not merely live to work anymore. I want to make a family with you, I want to take walks on the boardwalk with you, and I want to make love to you in that shower with the stars overhead. I want to dream and believe again. I want to hope and play. I want a real life, with you. The simple question is—Do you love me?"

Her answer sobbed out. "Yes, I do." Damn him, she had always loved him, all her life.

He was crazy, giving up everything he'd worked so hard to win.

With joy lighting his face, Matt pulled her into his arms and slipped the ring on her finger. "You've always been my Katie. Tell me yes. Tell me you're mine. Tell me you'll marry me."

He kissed her so sweetly and tenderly she nearly burst into new tears.

"Oh, Matt." She cupped his face and kissed him back.

Crackling lightning flashed, thunder banged and rolled, and Matt and Katie both flinched.

"That one was close." He grinned sheepishly.

She stroked his cheeks, studying his love shining there in his eyes, past and present. She wanted to believe they had a hope. She wanted to believe in Matt. He wasn't Jeb. Jeb had never quite grown up, and Matt had been an adult too long. Could they truly make a future out of this crazy tumble into love?

She'd never know if she didn't try.

Thunder rattled impatiently, as if urging her on.

"I love you. Yes, I'm yours, and you've always been mine. Yes, I'll marry you."

Relief and joy filled his face.

She sank into his impassioned kiss and wrapped her arms around him, holding on tight. "I'm sorry I've been so afraid. You made me feel again. You made me want and hope again. I was terrified."

"Aw, Katie."

The breeze gusted, tossing the curtains, and the rain poured.

Her fear had caused such a close call. If she'd lost him . . .

Between more needy kisses, she tackled his buttons and he stripped off his shirt.

Rain pounded and rushed on the roof, merging with the rolling thunder. In the dark of the storm, her room felt like their own sheltered island. At the next intense flash and boom, the clock blinked out.

He caught the hem of her T-shirt, and she raised her arms for him to slip it over her head, wincing briefly at having chosen to wear her oldest top and yoga pants today of all days. But her plans had been for serious thinking and decisions and a little wallowing in self-pity at her keyboard, not this—

Matt sucked in a sharp, admiring breath and skimmed his hands over her to cup her bare breasts, scattering kisses.

Matching him kiss for kiss, laughter swelling, she wriggled and tugged to slip down her pants. Matt helped, pulling them free from her feet, without breaking his raining kisses. She tackled his shorts next, loving his groan as she freed him.

Both now finally, delightfully naked, Matt gathered her into a hug, a perfect body-to-body hug, wrapping her in cherished feeling. Oh, no longer alone, no longer alone.

Outside, lightning flashed and burst over the

bay. The rain lashed down in ever-harder sheets.

He caressed her back. "I bet our puddle's filled up. Want to go wading?"

"No!" She laughed.

She had better plans. After a lingering caress of his ready erection, she stretched away to the night table and snatched a condom from the drawer. She turned back to Matt and pulled his mouth to hers for an impatient, needy kiss.

Then she pushed him back and opened the small package. He reached for the condom, but she shook her head. She leaned down to kiss him, closing her mouth over him for a brief tease before she leisurely covered his shaft, enjoying his long gusty groan.

Quick as a wink, he had her flipped around onto her knees, with her hands on the footboard, his hands tight on her hips, and he was filling her, deliberate and so deep. Slow in, slow out, he caressed her breasts, back, and shoulders. She shivered, soaking in the exquisite, tight friction as she looked out at the storm. He slipped a hand between her legs, long fingers stroking, jolting her with sensation, sweet and intense.

She gasped. "Oh, again. More."

The rumbling storm, the pouring rain, the cool breath of the breeze, the electric thrill of the lightning, the exquisite internal electricity his every steady stroke was raising in her, so much to feel, all joining into her own rising sensual tempest. Shivers prickled her skin, her breath raced.

Almost. So near. She arched into his hand, pressing into his next hard stroke. "Matt, oh, Matt!"

"I love you Katie. So beautiful. I can feel you so

tight around me, I can feel you coming."

Then, in time with the next crack of thunder, she did, flying sharply, perfectly apart in his arms.

~*~

Matt held Katie tight, supporting her trembling arms against collapsing as she caught her breath. Still stroking into her, easy and gentle, he enjoyed every ripple of her body around his.

Yes, this way felt incredible, but he needed to see her face, wanted to see her dimpled smile, and most of all, wanted to tell her again how much he loved her while looking into her eyes.

"Let's shift here." He withdrew and her frustrated groan left him undeniably smug.

She rolled onto her back, tugging him to her.

He stretched out over her, pressing up on his arms to drop slow kisses to her smiling lips and her dimple. Tracing his lips over her everywhere, loving her little shivers and breathy gasps. To delay and steady himself, he licked and suckled at her breasts, until he could wait no longer.

Lightning lit the room. Rain roared. Thunder banged and rolled overhead.

Gripping her hips and lifting her, he sank into her tight welcoming heat, slowly, looking into her loving eyes. He groaned from the pleasure, loving her smile, loving her sweet moans.

She bit her lip, raising her chin. "Oh, there, yes, Matt. There." She caught her hands onto his arms.

He leaned down to take her mouth again, tongues stroking together as he stroked into her body. Rocking together easy and peaceful, her body clenching and drawing at his, he wanted to draw out this intimate moment as long as their bodies would permit.

Her breath caught, and she shivered around him with a kitten cry. Determined to bring her up and send her over pleasure's edge once again, he gulped for breath, kept himself in check, and continued moving slow and steady.

Her smile bloomed. "I love you."

"And I love you." Amazing how those words came so easily now. What a fool he'd been for forgetting to add his love for her into all that nonsense of logic he'd plead on Sunday. Love was the answer, and he'd been so blind to the ease of the solution.

Another sharp crack again made them both start and laugh, but the loud storm couldn't disturb the new peace filling him.

"This is a great thunderstorm. Like when we were kids."

"I think they were great *because* we were kids. Storms were marvelous things to us, more than just agitated air colliding. So much held wonder back then, sunsets and tides and even the gulls on the wind. That boy."

"That girl." He smiled. "And new wonders now."

She rolled her hips, and that small movement tipped the balance. The pleasure overpowering, he had to shift and break away from kissing her, and rear up to raise her hips high and sink hard to the hilt. So good. Again, fast, and faster.

"Oh, Matt, yes, more." She fisted the sheets, his ring glittering on her hand, lifting, rising, clasping him tightly.

His Katie.

Sweating in the heavy air, breaths rushing, they rode together, hearts drumming along with the thunder. Another flash and boom, and drumming roll, and another flash, lighting Katie straining beautifully beneath him.

"Matt, please. I need."

So did he, his body and hers both demanded the time was now, time to move, time to take, time to give. Her legs shook and breath sobbed.

The pinging of hail mixed into the downpour.

He gasped. "Come on, Katie, let it come. Let me see you fly. I love you. You're so beautiful."

Lightning sparked and flared. Katie came sweet and hard, and the convulsive grip of her release shot him over the edge into his own. His shout and the thunder and Katie's, "I love you!" mixed into the wrenching burst of joyous relief.

She held him tight and close. Home, he'd come home in so many ways.

"I love you Katie. I've always loved you. I'll always love you."

As they cuddled in exhausted contentment, the thunderstorm moved out to sea, and the rain eased from pounding drum to a gentle whisper.

The happy elderly couple at the Seaward Inn drifted into his mind. Someday, Katie and he would be that couple. He had so much to look forward to between now and then, sharing a lifetime with Katie.

Long peaceful moments later, Katie stirred and glanced at the dark clock. "The power's still out."

He grinned. "A good excuse to laze around in bed."

"True." She leaned up on one elbow, tender

worry drawing her brows together. "Are you completely sure you don't want that partnership in Atlanta? We can work something out. I can't let you lose any of your dreams."

"Katie, second only to loving you, I've never been more certain of anything in my life. You even told me on Sunday. If I had really wanted one of those partnerships, I would have already decided. I didn't, nowhere as much as I imagined. What I do want now and forever is you, and once I understood that, deciding took no time at all."

He brushed damp tendrils of hair away from her cheek.

The sun broke through the clouds and spattering rain, flooding the room with light.

"I finally did the right thing in my life—I followed my heart and came home to you, my girl next door."

The End

Thank You!

Thanks for reading *Kissing Katie*. I hope you enjoyed it!

Would you like to know when my next book is available? You can sign up for my e-mail list at http://www.babettejames.com/Newsletter.

You can also connect with me online at http://www.babettejames.com, follow me on Twitter http://twitter.com/BabetteJames, or like my Facebook page http://facebook.com/BabetteJamesAuthor.

I would appreciate it if you would help others enjoy this book, too.

Recommend it. Please help other readers find this book by recommending it to friends, readers' groups and discussion boards.

Review it. Reviews help readers find books and I appreciate all reviews.

You've just read the first book in my His Girl Next Door Series. The other books in the series are *Convincing Cami* (Coming January 13, 2015), *Tempting Tessa* (Coming 2015), and *Loving Lexi* (Coming 2015). I hope you enjoy them all!

If you'd like to read an excerpt from *Convincing Cami*, please turn the page.

Coming Soon

Here's an excerpt of CONVINCING CAMI, Book 2 in the His Girl Next Door Series by Babette James.

Coming January 13, 2015

Good thing high school teacher Jack O'Malley likes a challenge. When his best friend's sister-in-law Cami Alexander moves next door, it's time for Jack to concede the sweet and sexy teacher is more than a long-time friend—she's the one he's been looking for in all the wrong places. He's ready to put his footloose bachelor days behind him and make his move, but between his past, Cami's doubts, her overprotective family, and well-meaning blind date offers from friends, convincing Cami they're meant to be together gets complicated.

Cami is willing to admit she's always had a little crush on the dashing, blue-eyed Jack. However, when the heat in a spontaneous kiss surprises them both, she's afraid to risk their friendship over mere desire. She's been burned by love before. But passion admitted turns irresistible, and one explosive night raises the stakes on their dilemmas. Jack vows his love and to stand by her through every trouble, but what if he's already broken that promise?

THE OLD WOODEN LADDER CREAKED AND ROCKED WITH loose joints as Cami climbed. The thing must be as old as the house. She stretched, screwing in the first bulb. The step under her feet creaked, cracked—

And gave way. She shrieked, dropping the light bulb, but grabbed only air. Oh, this was going to hurt—

"Cami!" Jack shouted. Strong arms caught her tight. "I got you."

Shaken from the close call, she sagged against him. "Thanks. That was too close."

"I knew I should have brought my ladders over. You okay?"

"Yes. Just a scare."

He let her slide to the floor, but held her snug against his body. He would release her, any second now. She should step away. Instead, she wrapped her arms around his waist. She shivered, this time less from the scare and more from realizing just how tightly he held her. How he'd never actually touched her before beyond a social hug or handshake.

Her quiet little crush speared into a hot rush of want. How warm and sturdy he was. How perfectly they fit together.

She caught her breath and looked up to find Jack studying her with puzzled, serious expression that she'd never seen on his face before. The twilight added a deceptive privacy to the dim room and made Jack's eyes appear dark and deep with—

Desire?

"This is a really bad idea," Jack muttered. Tightening his arms, he crushed his mouth down on hers.

She gasped, and he seized full advantage of her mouth opening under his in the hungry, demanding kiss.

Oh, Jack was right, this was a really bad idea, but the surprising kiss was far too amazing to rally any effort to break away. With the curiosity of six years pressing her, Cami recklessly surrendered to the pleasure, not caring he had a girlfriend, not caring they'd just careened over the friendship line . . . and his warm body was hard against hers.

What a kiss! Far from a perfect kiss—too hot and rushed—but wonderful, wonderful, fierce, and toe-curling.

Curiosity killed the cat, remember.

Well, she wasn't a cat, and this was just a kiss.

Right?

~*~

Available Now

Here's an excerpt of SUMMERTIME DREAM, Book 1 in The River Series by Babette James.

The Fourth of July is over, but for these summer lovers, the fireworks have just begun.

An unexpected inheritance brings business consultant Christopher Gordon from Los Angeles to quaint Falk's Bend. He's carved time from his demanding schedule to dispose of his great-grandparents' home and explore his roots. However, disturbing family secrets and the sweet temptation of writer Margie Olsson derail his plans, challenging him to seize the elusive dream missing from his hectic life—love.

A recent brush with death shook Margie's life, but not her dreams, and she's ready to move forward. Only, standing up to her loving, over-protective family isn't easy. Helping Christopher explore the derelict mansion and unravel his grandmother's mysterious past allows a fun taste of independence. But when her experimental summer fling ignites into unexpected love, can her small town dreams work with his big city life?

THE FOURTH OF JULY IN FALK'S BEND, Missouri, made pretending nothing ever changed almost possible, Margie Olsson decided. All it took was a dollop of stiff determination and a generous application of wishful thinking.

Even the arguments remained the same.

"Told you we'd be late." Her brother Joe wrenched open the hatch to their restaurant's minivan, the tight muscle in his jaw sending his mustache twitching.

Most of the townsfolk had finished migrating from the parade route to River Edge Park and claimed their favorite picnic table or stretch of ground. Now they swarmed the softball field and concession stand, ready to enjoy the town's 132nd annual Independence Day game.

Unperturbed at Joe's grouching, Dad hefted the massive pan of beans. "Why rush to sit and stew in a long line of cars? It's not like anyone would take our table. Plus, we can take our time unloading." With that, he trundled off to the large brick grills.

Joe's frown sharpened into a scowl that would do one of their Viking ancestors proud. "We could always try getting here early!" he growled at Dad's back and dragged out the largest ice chest.

Margie choked off a laugh. Some things had remained absolute over her twenty-four years of life: Dad would never arrive early to any event and Joe would always fuss like a mother hen.

"At least you have a sunny day for the game." She patted Joe's shoulder. "Cooler than last week, don't you think? I don't think we've had a more sweltering end of June."

Joe nodded woodenly. "I got the rest. Go on and find Grandma and Grandpa. Looks like Mom got them here on time." He waved her off, as if she were still a preschooler tagging his heels. This, with his being ten years older, was a familiar feeling.

As soon as he turned his back, Margie scooped up the smallest ice chest and followed him to their table where Grandpa and Grandma Olsson's wicker picnic basket waited.

Unfortunately, facts trumped determination and wishful thinking. Not everything in Falk's Bend remained the same. The Heller family's traditional table stood conspicuously empty, as did the Frost family's table. Being spared the inevitable awkward encounters should be a relief, but the gossips would surely set to talking again, and the misery flashing over Joe's face lodged a knot in her throat.

She fell in beside him as he returned for the next load. Should she ask now? The timing wasn't perfect, but she had him alone. A glance over to Dad found him gabbing with the four elderly Mills brothers, who thrived on checkers and gossip while supervising the assorted dishes simmering on the grills. Over at the gate, a tall man in a white shirt paused, and rubbed the back of his neck as he scanned the confusion of tables, until Bert Mills hailed him over. They all shook hands like old friends, so maybe he was the grandnephew expected down from Montana.

Margie blew at her bangs. Cooler weather was debatable. The heavy air clung like a steamy second skin and the flags, bunting, and bows draped the park as perky as wet laundry.

"Hey, Joe, I was thinking, I'd really like to get back to work on Monday." She winced at her blurt. Although Aunt Ida handled the staff schedules and Dad was the official boss, Joe ruled the family's restaurant these days and he'd be the hardest nut to crack in her effort to return to normal life.

"Aw, Margie, we agreed you'd use the time to rest up and write and start when Amy headed back to school in August."

"Come on. At least part time. I'm totally fine

now. I miss working—" She stumbled over a rough grass tuft.

Joe steadied her, his face strained and gaze darting over her. "You all right, sweetie? Maybe you should just take it easy today."

Oh, that snapped her last straw. "I'm fine! I'm weary to pieces with hearing 'Take it easy.' Dr. Saylor said no restrictions. I can do what I want. When I want. Anything!"

"Hey, Margie? Joe?" Her best friends Debi and Baxter strolled up beside Joe.

Joe planted his hands on his hips, another lecture looming. "Margie, I know, but—"

She crossed her arms against the chill surge of shame at losing her temper in public and her throat tightened. "No! Enough! You've got work to do. I'll see you after the game."

Grumbling under his breath, Joe stomped off.

Baxter dropped his bag on the table and stooped to kiss Debi quick and hard. "Hon, I'll go on help Joe unload. See you at the bleachers." He winked at Margie and loped after Joe.

Mirth sparkling in her blue eyes, Debi hugged Margie. "Well, well, there's hope for you after all! I've never seen you back Joe down before."

"He's just...being Joe. I shouldn't have snapped at him." Margie groaned. The giddy spark at having stood up for herself fizzled. Thank goodness, her parents had missed her tantrum. Joe hadn't been himself since breaking up with Stephanie and jumping down his throat was a dumb way to get his agreement.

"I've known you since the first day of kindergarten, and yeah, Joe means well, but let me tell you, that was one long overdue snap. I'm proud of you."

"I just wish he'd stop hovering." Margie peeked over her shoulder at the minivan. Baxter had Joe's softball gear, and Joe hauled out the first large, food-laden hotbox.

"Maybe you ought to think about a place of your own. You need a change."

"I've had enough change over the last year."

Debi waved her hand in a stop-it motion. "A positive change. And, yes, I know all the reasons why you stay with them. Heck, I'd leave Baxter for your mom's peach pancakes alone. But it's something you should consider seriously."

"I will. Someday." Even moving out wouldn't stop their loving, smothering concern.

"Why don't we skip the game? I'll crack open the pinot grigio and we can compare brotherly pet peeves."

Margie laughed. "I think we've covered them all over the years. Go on. Catch up with Baxter. Let me jot some quick scene notes, then I'll meet up with you all." That was a complete fib, but her skin crawled with the need for some space.

Debi accepted her fib with a commiserating hug and headed for the ball field.

Margie escaped for her favorite place in the park, the huge old oak topping the low rise of land between the picnic area and the ball field, with a perfect view of the game and the lazy river. Oh, thank goodness, she had the shady homemade swing to herself. She settled against the swing's thick rope, kicked off her sandals, and let out a heavy breath. Two sparrows squabbled and chased overhead through the shifting patterns of leafy shadow and sunlight. Drawing her bare feet up onto the heavy board polished smooth by years of bottoms and feet, she fluffed the skirt of her sundress over her knees. Determined to change her fib and mood around, she opened the story on her tablet and set to her note-making, resisting the urge to aimlessly edit.

Wild cheers jolted her attention to the game. Whoa. Seven innings already and tied at nine runs each. She sighed. Her missing the game would just give Joe one more thing to fuss over.

They all meant well, but when would Joe and everyone accept she was perfectly fine, better than ever, actually, and stop trying to keep her packed in cotton balls?

Patience, patience. All you can do is wait.

"Wait for what?" a quiet male voice answered.

Jolted, she sat straight, straddling the board to keep from falling, her heart zipping. She'd spoken out loud?

"Sorry, didn't mean to startle you." The man from the gate stood at the edge of the shade. "Just came over to check out this great old oak. I'll leave you be."

His soft, low voice, rich and warm as caramel, set every dormant feminine nerve on alert.

But who was he? Between growing up in Falk's Bend and working at the restaurant, she knew everyone and their kin, or, at least about them. If he was a Mills, he must take after his mother's family. He had the greenest eyes she'd ever seen set in a craggy, captivating face, and smile crinkles by his eyes and mouth. He was lanky and fit, but not so tall as Joe, and maybe older, late thirties. His sleek brown hair was neatly trimmed, his white polo shirt set off his outdoor tan, and more men should look as good in jeans as he did. Her gaze returned to those remarkable eyes of his, and something hot and bright leapt inside her.

He cleared his throat, as if he'd been waiting for a reply.

Holy moly. Heat flooded her. She'd been staring like an idiot. So that's what all that being lost in a man's eyes in romance novels felt like. Holy moly indeed.

~*~

Available Now

Here's an excerpt of CLEAR AS DAY, Book 2 in The River Series by Babette James.

What's a girl to do when her summer lover wants forever?

Haunted by dark memories of her parents' volatile marriage, artist Kay Browning keeps her heart locked behind a free-spirit facade and contents herself with the comfortable affair she has every summer with easygoing photographer Nate Quinn.

The only trouble with her plan? This summer Nate's come to Lake Mohave to claim the lover he can't let go. He's done with the endless traveling and settling for temporary homes and temporary loves. Kay's always been more than just a vacation fling, and now he must convince this woman, who sees love as a course to certain heartbreak, to take that leap of faith and learn how safe love with the right man can be.

OF COURSE, THE MORE SHE DETERMINED NOT TO think of Nate, the more she did.

"Just perfect." Kay Browning tipped her Dodgers cap low against the mid-morning glare and kicked into a hard backstroke through the cool water. Blue skies, hot July sun, intense desert landscape—another perfect day at Lake Mohave. Except for the futile if-onlys snarled in her mind like fishing line.

Nate Quinn had come along with July and Mohave for the past six years. He'd sail in like a freshening wind, they'd share two weeks of fishing, playing, and loving, Kay's careful schedule demolished to a pleasant shambles, and then he'd be off again on his adventures. Kay's life would resume its organized pace, punctuated by glossy postcards, scattered bursts of e-mails, IMs and silly tweets, the occasional twenty-plus-page letter, and the odd oblivious-to-time-zone phone call.

Kay liked how they kept the relationship simple. No demands on each other. No clinging, pining or carping. A happy, mutual understanding: she stayed and he went. But this summer, however much she hated admitting the feeling, Nate's absence threw off her sense of balance.

No whining, no pining, remember? She turned with a splash, adjusted her cap, and swam hard toward shore.

Life happens. Focus on what you can control.

At the moment, that was her painting.

She allowed herself one heavy sigh. Why every last one of her friends had inexplicably cancelled on the set-in-stone annual vacation—well, plans change. As for Nate . . . She hadn't pined over anything since she was ten. This was simple, annoying regret.

She coasted into the shallows, rolled to her back and forced herself to relax and float. In her mind's eye she drew Nate sitting there on the beach with the sun-drenched background of stark rocky land and softening tangles of willow, mesquite, and tamarisk, and the mental exercise halfway worked in distracting the fidgets—as long as she kept her eyes closed. Fantasizing wasn't pining. Quick pencil strokes to block him in. Slower, surer on the details. He liked his blond hair in a crew cut. His lean shoulders, strong, long hands . . . She trailed her fingertips over his favorite path from her waist over her ribs upward to—Nope, no fantasizing that way. Back to drawing. Maybe she'd grab a sketchpad later and work out a few real drafts.

Lips set together, relaxed, with the faintest lift of a smile at the corners. The faint crook to his rugby-broken nose. His agile, comic eyebrows lay thick and straight over gray eyes. His ears stuck out a charming slightest bit. Beautiful cut abs and pecs proved his claims of laziness a lie. A perfect amount of body hair dusted silky crisp over chest, arms and legs. Men were such texture contrasts: the satin of skin and rasp of hair, jut of bone and arc of muscle, soft lips and calloused fingers. He wouldn't have shaved yet today, and there would have been sandpapery-rough morning kisses. She almost heard him calling her, "Hey, Kay!" in the relaxed, husky way he—

With a splash, she erased the frustrating daydream. This wishful imagining fixed nothing. Her sheltered little camp would still be empty. Should she give in, pack up the camp, and hit the road north to Lake Mead instead? Just break her routine for once.

No, but it was definitely past time to get her tush out of the water and do something constructive. This lonely gnawing in her bones and brain was unacceptable. Kay pushed to her feet, facing out to the scenic lake created out of a stretch of the Colorado River and the rugged land beyond shimmering with heat.

Work, right, but it was too early in the day for the hard afternoon light she needed for the Coyote

Point painting. She was too restless to read or fish and not in the mood to take the boat over to the marina, chat with George, and buy ice.

She rolled her shoulders and stretched, enjoying the hot air licking over her wet skin. As she wiggled her feet in the sand and gravel-bottomed shallows, a flurry of minnows darted past her ankles, and her silver toe ring glinted beneath the clear water. She paused, caught by the possibilities in the sparkling sun on water and the intricate, shifting reflections over gravel. Yes! Exactly the distracting challenge she needed. Shaking the water from her ears, she pivoted toward camp.

"Kay!" That male voice was not her imagination.

"Oh, shit!" She twisted and dropped into the water, sinking neck-deep. Mother always said, among other things, that a lady never goes skinny-dipping and must always wear a proper hat. Kay was only half skinny-dipping, but she fervently wished she'd worn something a bit more substantial than a baseball cap and the bottom half of the quintessential teeny-weenie yellow polka-dot bikini.

Shit, oh, shit, oh, shit. She so hated when Mother was right.

Okay, time to find out who'd just gotten an eyeful. The guy had called her name, so she should know him. Oh boy, if she'd flashed old George . . .

She wiped water from her face, sucked in a breath against her pounding heart, and peeked around.

Nate.

She must be sun-dazed. Nate? With a beard? Hair curling over his ears? No way. Just because a familiar slouchy fishing hat topped those unruly, sun-bleached blond curls and just because this guy possessed the same deep-water tan and footloose taste in clothes as Nate with his electric blue Hawaiian shirt, bright orange swim trunks, and beat-up deck shoes didn't mean—

"Hey, babe. Now that I've finally caught your attention, how about a hug from my girl?" He opened his arms. "Am I coming in after you or are you coming out?" Only Nate's voice held that mellow timbre like chocolate for her ears.

"Nate! What…" Giddy delight flushed over Kay, clearing her shock. She dashed from the water and into strong arms, a wonderful hug, and a better kiss that launched her mind into a blissed-out whirl of *oh, yes* and *why*?

The *oh, yes* won out until the need to breathe forced them apart.

Nate gave her a long look, his usually easy gray eyes holding a new, simmering heat.

Wow. Whoa.

His slow hands followed the trail of his roving gaze: gentle tracing of cheek and lips, gliding across hips, waist and ribs, and grazing over her breasts to cup and caress. With his tender, simple touches, he stirred the warm desire of her daydream into full need. She shut her eyes, soaking in the unexpected pleasure. *Oh, yes.*

~*~

About the Author

Babette James writes sweetly scorching contemporary romance and loves reading nail-biting tales with a satisfying happily ever after. When not dreaming up stories, she enjoys playing with new bread recipes and dabbling with paints. Babette is a member of New Jersey Romance Writers, Romance Writers of America, Contemporary Romance Writers, Celtic Hearts Romance Writers, and Liberty States Fiction Writers. As a teacher, she loves encouraging new readers and writers as they discover their growing abilities. Her class cheers when it's time for their spelling test! Born in New Jersey and raised in Southern California, she's had a life-long love of the desert and going down the shore. Babette lives in New Jersey with her wonderfully patient husband and extremely spoiled cats.

www.ingramcontent.com/pod-product-compliance
Lightning Source LLC
Chambersburg PA
CBHW071232130626
46556CB00003B/981